Helen and Robert Porter

# RIVER'S END
## *and Other Stories*

# RIVER'S END

*and*

*by*

MC DOWELL, OBOLENSKY

# Other Stories

### Anthony C. West

 **NEW YORK**

823.91
W 516 ri

ACKNOWLEDGMENT is here made to *Esquire, The Magazine For Men,* in which the following stories in this volume first appeared: "The Turning Page," "Narcissus Unto Echo," "Not Isaac," "Song of the Barrow," and the title story, "River's End."

# Contents

# RIVER'S END
## *and Other Stories*

# River's End

As SCALES ON a golden basking fish the sun laid his light across the waste of bog that rimmed the horizon with a plain of leathery shimmering brown. Gravid with heat a beech drowsed by the schoolhouse window, green-glossy and replete. Fullness was the day's destiny and summer's redolent fullness lay upon the land asleep in warmth. And so it would sleep until the birds held evensong and cooling twilight uncurled a breeze to set the leaves whispering, dancing into summer's night.

Along the bog the river browsed its curving banks that were self-sculpted to its flowing, molded by the floods of spring to rounded forms of clay and peat that were to water as print on sand is to the foot, or wind's wild image cut on bunkers of snow; the drowsy gurgling water taking the peat's tincture and running on with but a purl and lazy vortex here and there over a feather-smooth bed of soft mud, forgetting the stone-chatter and white frill of mountain burn; on and on, finding washed sand and taking its sun-yellowness until at last it met its end and died into the living sea. Someday, Stephen thought, he would go along the stream, following faithfully each curve and

3

bend until he found the ocean too; and westward then across it to far lands, finding another river mouth and following to its source, a wet-lipped crack in rock under a sheet of snow. . . .

Framed perfectly by the window frame there was a broken fence, a tumbling wall of stone, a tall hawthorn hedge darkly green, its May-magic now seedling haws, the sloping corner of a field where a black cow grazed with her calf. . . .

"Stephen? What is the Gaelic for summer?"

The bald question seared his dreaming like a hot iron, thumb-pressing into his mind the word, dream and woman, and ever after giving a concrete symbol for the time, circumstance and season; not without qualm for death was present, too, and error. . . .

Miss Ross had read his mind and he blushed, as far as it went not resenting the trespass, but blushing since she had seemed to catch an ill-made dream that lay with others not so fit for capture.

His dark expressionless eyes stared into the teacher's pale blue ones as if in turn he tried to read what she was reading. The girl had to look away, making an excuse by checking another child for talking, not pressing the question and unable to return to it as a teacher should because she knew his eyes still rested on her.

Stephen saw her on the high stool before the class as he had seen her many a day in one dress or another. This day more aware he noticed she was lightly clad against the heat, nothing on her shoulders but a skin-thin blouse through which he could mark the intimate ribbons of her undergarments—a pink ribbon and a green one lying over

her shoulders; the pink supporting her slip and the green
holding up her vest; fair-haired, wholesome, and clean in
body, but plain in pock-marked face, the hair's sheen accentuating the sallowness of cheek and neck; mature with
small, low breasts that only shaped a little on her chest, so
tightly pressed against the ribs they were as if her strong
sense of chastity wished to disguise them altogether like a
nun; her pale white forearms, wearing much finer skin
than her features, crossed on her lap; her heels caught up
on the stool's worn rung, thighs foreshortened by her pose
as if she knelt upon her heels, barelegged and cool on
moist grass in tree shadow or a prow's profile gliding forward on sun's great incandescent waves, poised above a sea
emotionlessly; a galleon's prow laden with fantastic treas-
ure bound surely for a shore that waited for the gentle
give and take of tide. . . .

"Well, Stephen?"

Shuddering, he shook off the persistent dream and
frowned to make-believe cogitation, but never moved his
eyes although they now saw little save his own ignorance
for her question.

Under his seeless gaze Miss Ross blushed as if the
first warm wave of his nameless passion had now only
reached her. Self-consciously, she moved her arms. He saw
her blush and blushed hotly in turn, guilt giving her keen
discovery much as a felon makes long the law's arm.

His loose imaginings seemed unlawful: his love for
river, rockscape, marsh, and hawk's spiral heathen leanings
far beyond the parish Decalogue; that he should laugh for
the mad expectancy of a March day when the sun made
cathedral lights under great cumulus or weep on the

finality of a December sunset were tolerable signs of sac-
rilegiousness, even to his mother who knew the time-tried
poets and encouraged his interest in them: God lived in
church and spoke from the parson's mouth while unshriven nature reeved and roved wantonly outside, seasons
no more than changes of clothes and sowing and harvest-
ing; spring lamb time and autumn ram time.

The other twenty-odd children had now caught the unseen intercourse, puzzled by the tangible, tense silence and
looking from teacher to Stephen and back again, and he
could feel their weight as they jostled for a place of van-
tage. Being older by two years than any of them save Anne
Stafford and being thrice as articulate, he knew he had
more authority inside and out of school than had Miss
Ross and he was aware she admitted this, implying he
should help her and much as a monitor keep the larger
unruly ones in hand.

His eye flickered sideways to Anne. She stayed aloof,
eyeing her teacher resentfully although the latter's twenty-
three gave the girl seven clear years. But Anne's contours
were full and finished and mocked the girlish clothes
upon which her stubborn parents insisted, refusing to
admit that abstract days by a calendar might well have
slight relationship to the reality of maturity; he knew they
were ambitious for their daughter, wanting her to become
a teacher as his own ambitious parents aimed him: while
Anne might well qualify, he knew he never would, for
the sake of peace going through the motions while only
marking time, the marking not unpleasant; the only real
ambition the future stirred in him was to own a knapsack
and wander through valley and over hill in this or any

other land, beauty, sunwarmth and starshine his incre-
ment.

Little in the big parish escaped him: at first hand he
knew his neighbors within a five-mile radius of his home,
their ways and habits and the over-all rigid law that
guaranteed the proprieties. The honest nature of his case
with Anne Stafford, like all of nature's pleasant pleading,
was out of the parish court; that grown-up boys and girls
held hands in summer lanes or danced together under
adult patronage was prelude to marriage: while tinkers
and poor-whites might whore on ditches, no self-respect-
ing yeoman Protestant, bearer of the proud heritage of
the Reformation, dare take a woman minus parson's sanc-
tion. This was the parish law that Stephen knew, and
teacher, parson and parent obeyed it.

One girl he knew, a pretty girl and strong farmer's
daughter, had got herself a child and ever since she seldom
went out, hiding her child at home, her people shamed
and ostracized as well, the bastard's father emigrating.
Quite well he knew these things and yet their very solidity
teased him to ignore them and reach for sensations which
the law named carnal sin.

He knew Miss Ross was very holy, sooner to sing hymns
than any man-made song of life, love or patriotism: God's
and parson's patriot she was, making no secret of it, although he had overheard some of the single males, who
invariably gossiped to the bell's last clang outside church
on Sunday mornings, confess as they watched the prim
teacher walk over the noisy gravel into the church porch
with sedate prayer book in gloved hand that they would
rather try to bed a nun, naming her assistant second cur-

ate, even though she earned three hundred pounds a year, which was as much cash as five small farms could scrape off acid soil.

Idly he wondered if Miss Ross was ever lonely or if in God she had a friend, sweetheart, companion, father . . . a great queen bee brown as its own furred humming soared into the schoolroom and ranged with arrogant summer note in wide powerful spirals and Stephen saw again his summer day as if the beesong were its signature and exact symbol, and ever after if a bee mistook a February's half hour of false summer sun and crossed his path with droning flight he saw again the schoolhouse and its figurehead, Miss Ross.

The bee bundled against the windowpane, its wing song sharpening with frustration as it met the glass, purring from bottom to top of the pane and dropping back baffled, hurting its wings, its legs thick with pollen's ocher, unable to sense the air's freedom a bare inch above its invisible barrier.

Fooney Murray, the school's fool, got excited and pointed to the bee, laughing and saying, "Bee! bee! Stephen!" over and over, looking to Stephen to set the prisoner free.

Stephen made a warning face at the big boy who, had he his full wits, was man-strong and grown. Without the wits he was zany-gentle and impressionable with an atavistic attraction for dead things like mice or birds, hoarding them when he found them in his pockets until they smelled and finally dried themselves to shoddy mummies. Feeling the bee's incarceration as much as Fooney, Stephen took a curve of blotting paper and shoveled the insect outside, watching it for the moment it picked up flight and burned away, its anthem fading. . . .

"What is the Gaelic for bee, Stephen?" Miss Ross smiled and the children laughed at last, getting the hang of the game. He breathed relief now, knowing she had seen nothing in him more than an attitude of dream for summer and a bee.

Claiming no measure of sanctity himself, he knew that saintliness in others might very often illuminate another's wickedness and he would not have denied her had Miss Ross claimed a pinch of second sight.

His gaze broke from her face and sought where Anne was playing with a pencil, her proud young breasts gathered up between her forearms in spite of clothes or parents. Fooney was still muttering about the bee and he saw again the boy gibbering impotently at a ring of brazen girls unmercifully baiting him, undoing for fun his trousers and screaming excitedly at his man-sized genitals, Fooney shouting, "Stephen, save me!"

And the laughing struggle with Anne over the cretin's cap, her small brown hands as quick and strong as his own. And then the cap ceased to be the struggle's reason, the wrestling itself reason until they fell laughing on the grass, his arms around her body and his hands accidentally on her breasts. He did not know if it was the sudden terrible softness of her breasts, his hands' intuition for them, or his eyes' sense for the glint of her naked powerful thighs exposed by the ruched dress, but struggle and laughter ceased and in amaze he felt excitement running through his body with greater strain than any scrimmage. Her hands let the cap go and her eyes caught his own, offering him cap and all else he might find in the rich cupboard of her maidenhood. And since then, an hour ago, thought bred with thought and offered no other solution but a man's in spite of reputation's hazard under the basilisk that was the unsleeping parish eye.

He himself took little umbrage for his youthfulness, knowing he was boy-free still and freer than a man with all of summer still hoarded in his hands, this sudden passion for the girl not confessing kith with either conscious love or lust, more personal and poignant but not much different to the satisfaction he would feel when lying naked in a warm shallow stream or wandering through the aisles of evening when every bird held up its torch of song.

Miss Ross did not and could not know a boy's mind but she had ears. Stephen memorized his request a dozen times between lunch and end of school, selecting and discarding as many suitable sites quite cunningly. By the cloakroom door he thought he whispered a time and place to the shy-willing, understanding girl, but because his heart boomed in his chest and drove his blood's breakers crashing on his eardrums his voice was loud and Miss Ross heard all.

She was indignant but did not know what to do, the physical size of the offenders limiting the free function of her authority, and knowing a girl past puberty was gifted with old knowledge that could spy the slightest movement in another woman's eye. Stephen she might handle, but the feline Anne. . . .

"Ridiculous!"

She flung the word away from her, rolling the r like small thunder over the empty, scraffled desks, not realizing the discovery's full shock until surreptitiously smoothing a whiff of powder on each cheek. Her hand trembled as she looked into the compact's mirror and saw, like Beauty's stepmother, Anne Stafford's rosy face instead of her own.

Unreasonably, she despised the girl, putting her mind's powers on the problem in earnest and remembering the little feline plays in school, the asking for a blotter, the pencils sharpened. . . .

She could not tell the Staffords what was afoot; ambitious, God-fearing parents like her own, whose hands were tender only for money and would crush without hesitation any wildflower or weed of lawlessness; hard work, hard cash, religion—the way laid down by Moses and Calvin so straight and narrow that to walk it half of life had to be left unlived. And the righteous Stafford would naturally blacken Stephen to whiten his daughter, the parish hand reaching for stones against the boy even as his great patron had been stoned. . . .

And she could not pass the discovery on to the rector, shrinking instinctively from the unmaidenly description of her fears for a sordid ending; and the rector would be quite impartial as a man, going harder on Stephen and not appreciating how the girl had dragged her common lure before the boy, nor aware how girls even as young as Anne Stafford were competent in the arts of enticement. . . .

Suddenly she saw the dusky evening when, seventeen, her father had whipped her for talking to a boy outside the gate. She had laughed with foreign, unpremeditated wantonness and the laugher had made the boy catch her and hold her tightly to him and then her father came and slashed her thighs and legs with a thin switch so she could not tell where caress ended and stinging pain began, the sensations living on and on with laughter into her dreams which neither parent nor prayer seemed able to restrain. . . .

Passion's solitary marker on the dull plate of memory —no love words, kiss, or caress—bodies held together, the boy nameless, sinless and without personality now and only a being of strength and substance holding her until her father chased her before him in shame, deep-shamed before the boy, self and parent; blood's rebellion crushed and cleansed by the long prayer they had prayed for her; kneeling by the bed she had fainted and they never knew, going out a while into some great freedom full of laughter, then coming back refreshed and quiet to hear her father's chanting voice. . . .

She shrugged uncomfortably, ashamed of this weak return to an irregular moment, seeing her father's solemn face and seeing God's iron face not unlike father's . . . *Our Father, name hallowed and will be done on earth.* . . .

But this she knew was always her melancholy hour with empty, silent room and children's distant laughter rolling like bright new coins along the gay roads home, her daily usefulness ended and nothing ahead save tea, a book, bed and prayers . . . Our Father in the heavens sternly denying all unrighteous parish pleasures. . . .

Mrs. Turley came in with broom, rag and pail and she remembered to warn the woman to have the schoolroom ready for an evening service the coming Sunday.

"Yes, miss," Turley replied almost with a curtsey, implying the task would be pure love-labor.

Miracles and immaculate conceptions excepted, she knew that two of Mrs. Turley's five wains had been born long after Mr. Turley leaped out of life by jumping off a runaway horse and cart. With the rector's consent, she had removed the widow from sin's sly environment by offering her the cleaner's job and empty school dwelling-house.

Gauged by the resonance of her amens, the bousy poor-white Turley's conversion was complete were it not for the slinking rumors that suggested her romantic life was nowhere near its close by entertaining in the evenings several slow neighboring farmers and laborers.

Jokers had twitted the attempted reclamation by fixing a hurricane lamp with red-painted glass to the schoolhouse chimney, although Miss Ross had never understood the exact significance of the scarlet sign, the rector forbearing to enlighten her when he had had it removed.

She watched the big, saucy woman at her work, humming out of all tune a hymn with conviction, the raw, round arms powerful as a man's, the great bosom straining the seams of a frock she herself had given, a pinch of surprisingly fine-skinned white breast squeezing itself out of a slit near the armpit. . . . And sadly she admitted failure.

Notwithstanding all she had done—all the prayers, clothes, occupation, decent instruction for the Turley off-spring—the brand still smoldered and not without coarse attractiveness and some honesty; all the well-meant intentions providing little more than a better house in which to sin: this humble refugee loudly hailing her God in church while whispering with the Devil round the corners and yet in grim poverty miraculously content, never refusing a weeping child a comforting word, laughter seldom far from the full lips, whereas a bleak smile on her saintly mother's mouth seemed a torture of indulgence....

Becoming angry with despondency and frustration and despairing of this labor tilting sexual windmills, she saw Turley, mother, Anne Stafford all one woman and all ill-balanced parts of herself, and the only unexciting way she might ever balance them would be to ape the three monkeys on her room's mantel shelf—see, hear, and speak no evil, walking through life with deaf ear and bowed head and even that left the fourth sense feeling quite unprotected. . . .

"Agh!" she said half-aloud impatiently as she went out, forgetting to say good-by to Turley who looked after her curiously. A good straightforward whipping would cure Anne Stafford's precocity and she could easily see herself raking the girl's round plump bottom with a rod until it matched her rosy cheeks for redness. . . .

Oblivious to the panorama of summer's mature beauty available to any eye from the schoolhouse steps she saw Stephen Muir throwing stones to dislodge the idiot's cap which for final gesture the departing girls had flung up into a tree.

She watched them, Fooney forgetting his cap and delighting in Stephen's prowess, cheering and dancing when the stones flew like birds through the air and scrabbling fresh ammunition off the road.

She frowned, unable to understand how such an arrogant boy could be so gentle and long-suffering for the fool whose slobbering mouth and deep, wide, wise-foolish eyes offended her and always smelling with his own sour smell and the odors of the dead things he carried jealously in his pockets. She shuddered, remembering the day she took a blackbird away from him. But for Stephen he might have attacked her, mouthing for his bird, calling it "Bawbee, bawbee" and saying Stephen would not marry her now for taking his bawbee away. She had flung it out of the window. Stephen had gone for it, returning it to Murray and himself holding the disgusting thing as if he loved it much as the fool.

"It may be dead, miss," he had muttered, "but to Fooney its yellow beak and glossy feathers are beautiful."

Next time she saw a blackbird for the first time she had noted how golden bright its bill in spite of her instinctive horror for all God's feathered creatures since, when a child, a cock-turkey had chased a red dress she wore for half a mile.

Stephen was smiling and talking to Murray. She knew he had qualities beyond the average run of small farmers' sons and instead of teacher she saw him as a parson, handsome, dark and tall in spotless surplice. . . .

The back tire of her cycle was flat. She could have inflated it herself, but she called the boy. He looked up, flung a last and lucky stone, clapped the cap on Murray's head and came obediently. She stood beside him as he pumped the tire.

"How do you like the Irish?" she asked conversationally, looking for an opening.

"All right, miss," he replied, putting the pump back on the frame and looking up, adding: "I think you've a slow puncture."

"It will take me home," she said, blushing a little in

spite of herself. He was taller than she was, boy-handsome with shadow of pup's down on his upper lip.

In friendliness, pity and some inward pain of unknown origins, her features tried to make a smile. In spite of youth and arrogance the boy seemed lost, lonely and friendless.

"You're not doing very well with the Irish?" she heard herself saying.

He nodded several times fatalistically.

"You must make an effort, y'know?"

He nodded again.

"It's essential you have it for exams. If you fail it—it rather reflects on me since you're really coming here to learn it."

He looked at the ground near her feet and she wished she could stop talking like a teacher, but his boy-world was a foreignness while her human-world was a narrow path between religion and good works.

"Stephen," she said protectively, putting a hand on his shoulder and wanting but unable to tell him baldly not to meet Anne Stafford.

He accepted the hand with but a slight half-inward twinge so that the girl nonsensically felt as if he had violently flung her hand away.

His eyes opened inquiringly at his name and in his shroud of obedient reserve she saw herself reflected and knew that coat, face, form and mind's supposed content had dubbed her spinster fifteen years before her time. It was sudden panic that tightened her fingers on his shoulder, her hand seeming to take comfort from the impersonal physical contact with a living human soul. . . .

"It is not true," she whispered to herself, letting her arm drop back and almost forgetting the boy.

She closed her eyes and Stephen thought she was saying a prayer as sometimes she was wont to do; perhaps she was praying for his better Gaelic. Unable to see female for teacher, yet he felt sorry for her and promised himself he would make better effort, guilty that his laziness caused her worry. Cycling slowly home he felt good and resolved until suddenly he remembered Anne Stafford.

Descendant of the track made by the feet of wild tribal men, the narrow road twisted and turned for no mechanical reason, making itself as long again; past the upper corner of the great peat bog with its knife-cut cliffs of turf where martins burrowed yard-long tunnels into the soft, rusty humus; down a short, sharp brae where the river threaded a bridge, trout shimmering slim shadows over the pebbles in the clear water and then moving away from his reflection with such life-full swiftness that the movement was vanishment, not motion; swallows raiding the gnats' miasma or gently scooping cups of water; on over the bridge and up a hill, fields one side, dense larch copse the other, and above the planted trees a wood of tall old beeches with smooth leaden boles where the sparrow hawks had bred for years, no keeper ever discovering them.

And again near home the road greeted the river that seemed to thread the parish through and through, lingering in it and reluctant to leave, making great loops and half-circles, doubling back, not fifty yards of it straight, sometimes narrow enough to leap and other times wide, but shallow enough to wade with dry feet, save in wet

season when it rose beyond its banks and sought to touch
again its ice-old margins up the hillsides when in Noah's
time it was mighty as an Amazon and surfeited with
melting snow.

Not wanting to start homework too soon on such a
halcyon afternoon he dawdled, his eyes seeing and drinking and all the time a third slow observer in his mind
seeing the meeting with Anne Stafford and making eyesight all the more satisfying, paradise completed by the
promised Eve.

He took his tea, his mother asking the volume of his
homework.

"Not much today," he lied, naming a chapter to be
read in history which he already knew and could pass
her testing easily.

"Well, do it when you finish tea," she said. "I've found
a poem you may like. It's by Shelley and's called 'Ode to
the West Wind.' It's long, but we can go over it in parts
and paraphrase as you go."

He nodded, glancing at the clock and estimating the
time.

After twenty minutes of history she opened her old
black leather-bound *Golden Treasury* with its gilded edges
and put on her glasses, looking up to see if he were ready
to listen, then starting to read in her chaste quiet voice
the wind's loud rhetoric.

Perforce, Stephen listened; then listened with interest,
his heart going faster. The poet had seen a wind's action
and movement as he had seen Irish winds in autumn from
which the dead leaves also fled, yellow and black and pale;
the stubble fields softly whining in the wind and shining

under a swift wind-driven moon, the hedges crouching and old reeds by the river whistling; wild spirit everywhere, destroyer and preserver. . . .

But weighted by expectancy the afternoon stayed still as if the sun burked his mission and hung above the anxious western sky for very spite. By road the rendezvous was a good four miles; by crow, something over two. He elected to go on foot and hovered unobtrusively about his home in case his father found a chore for him, edging further away until, when clear of human sight, he ran, striking an even flowing stride that matched breath, heartbeat and desire for, apart from its fulfillment, desire he now knew.

Down the last field above the cross he eased to a walk and wondered how he could use the time and place and girl and how she might react. She might rebuff him, intending only to talk. . . .

She would come along the road and would say, "Hello, Stephen," and smile or maybe laugh nervously. He would be nervous, too, but must not display it. He went back to the wrestling at school and saw again her solemn, ancient eyes, enheartened because he was only doing what mutely they had asked him to do. . . .

He would suggest that she walk with him and since there must be subterfuge they could not walk the open road. They would have to take to the quiet fields. There was a level, dry field with an old Celtic rath in a corner still fenced with dense blackthorns the Celts had used for stockade. Seldom did anyone go there and on the chief's high mound they could survey the road. That would be the place.

They would walk there, passing through the cattle gaps in the thorn, scramble up the steep rampart and sit down on the top. Anne would be sitting beside him. . . .

They might talk a little more and then he would move closer. . . . Maybe he should kiss her? No, that was silly. Firstly, he would lay gently a hand on her breast and if she accepted that, in a little while he would lay a hand on her thigh. . . .

His heart leaped into his throat as he reached the cross-roads. There was not a soul in sight, but he was early. Sitting on the gate's top bar he continued with his plan, but somehow the moment had passed and he could not proceed past lifting the girl's skirt. It seemed a mean thing to do and at the idea of it his desire died down, seeing again the bare defenseless thighs in the playfield and her shapeless blue knickers. . . .

Hard and judging as they were, the parish laws might well be valid. . . . But no, it was not that: these laws had never stopped him telling a lie or pinching apples or swearing or fighting or gaffing fish in restricted waters or hitting a cock-pheasant with a stone, or thinking what he wanted to think. This thing with Anne was like thinking aloud in a market place, like going naked in a street, and he might well get a child if he were able to get one and brand the girl for life and, worse, condemn himself to exile. . . .

And then a master feeling issued from his mind, greater than chip or parish rule on any shoulder or fear of shame for self, and greater than any beardless lust this girl might stir in him because her female parts matched him and were his opposite. He saw her with pity, seeing the pa-

thetic thighs again, the rough red ring of garters above
her knees, the tragic, ludicrous girl-woman's make-believe
as if she had something valuable to hide and the way she
moved and turned her head and hoped her movements
would be fetching; dimly his intuition groped in darkness
to grasp the mystery yet unknown behind the bare me-
chanics of a tupping, pity now tainted with faint disgust
and regret that the rendezvous had been made at all as if
he had already broken her and watched her lying at his
feet on the chief's mound, damaged and soiled like a dirty
handkerchief in a gutter. . . .

And the haunting ominous quality of Shelley's "Ode"
still lingered in his mind and lay weightless but heavily
over the evening and had to do with season's change and
earth's leaning to the sun. . . .

He lifted his eyes to the evening's fair face; cirrus lay
across the sky like gleanings on a hayfield and he had a
small regret as if summer were betrayed, one so well loved
but for a time not loved so well and undeserving of un-
faithfulness.

Here were his fields, hedgerows, trees, roads and winding lanes—all owned by strangers but by their foursquare
seasonal beauty vested in him. And the river, leaping
down steep screes until it reached the level parish, crossing its last fall above the Quarry Turn where men and
water had taken gravel for centuries, eating away the
hill's face and making a drop of a hundred feet down to
the deep pool that always swirled like tea in a cup where
trekking salmon slept at night; then sliding softly down
the vale, praised by willow, alder and saintly birch that

soaked their thirsty roots in its wetness and never knew the pain of drought.

He smiled, content again, remembering the old Celts believed that every river in the land was the mortal image of a goddess and his river was the goddess Annalee.

This was Thursday; come Saturday he would creep early away from home and follow the stream up into the hills again, climbing its dwindling course as it jumped from shelf to shelf of rock until its end, a little ever-running lake in an arid, upland valley far above the lush parish and even above its laws.

But his throat grew tight again for a bicycle carrying a female form bowled down the hill from Stafford's farm. He was nervous, now scared of the girl's eyes' lure, half-hooked still. Swiftly the cyclist came close.

It was not Anne Stafford and he was glad. It was Miss Ross. Steadying himself, he waited for her to speak and pass: "Good evening, Stephen," she would say and smile and primly nod her head and pedal on and he would touch his cap. . . .

But she did not pass, riding straight across the wide grass verge and bumping into a hidden stone and almost falling before she got off, the saddle point hitching up her dress to show two knobbly knees and slightly bandy thighs smothered in passionless gray bloomers. He looked away as she rearranged swiftly her skirt while laying the cycle on the grass, sensing her near fall had unnerved her, conscious of an embarrassed scorn-pity for her ineptitude; she seemed so knobbly and awkward with a simple bicycle. He noted too the sharp edge of her right shin had a rough six-inch weal where she had scraped it. He knew that such a scrape must sting, but she seemed to ignore it, looking at him and past him as if afraid to see him and saying unsmilingly: "Good evening, Stephen."

She closed her eyes a moment, savoring objectively the bright hard pain on her shin which made her a little weak, and for a moment hardly aware that hours had passed since she had talked to him outside the school porch while at the same time feeling a full century had elapsed.

He touched a grudging forelock and said, "Good evening, miss," as she walked toward him, marking she wore a fresh white dress patterned by long green fonds that moved on the material as weeds undulate in water, long loose sleeves of the diaphanous blouse tied at the wrists with green ribbons, the blouse deeply v'd at the neck, revealing a flat chest without a breast-valley as Anne's full breasts were valleyed, their secret hollow starting almost under her chin.

She seemed to him dressed up. Always neat and smart in school, she now appeared as if she had taken special care, her hatless hair no longer in a bun but gathered carefully into two flaxen whorls over her ears, each shell pinioned by numerous amber-colored hairpins.

From some dark corner in his ancestral mind the rising man in him observed her, judged and then discarded; apart from being teacher and her scrawny looks, his nonage placed her unfairly on a par with his mother and all the other adult women he knew. In deference to her status he dropped off the gate and stood before her, watching her forefingers play nervously with her thumbs, her injured leg bent at the knee and twitching slightly, her lips trembling.

"Stephen," she said softly yet urgently, calling his eyes to her face. "Anne—Anne Stafford isn't coming."

His face fell at the two-pronged thrust, his mind immediately lunging to the mystery of her discovery. He knew the light-speed of parish gossip which guilt trebled: had Anne confessed to someone, someone telling someone who told Miss Ross and Miss Ross telling old Stafford and Stafford running to rector and his father. . . . Else why should she bother to come all this way down past the Quarry Hill, the house she lodged in all of four miles away. . . .

Miss Ross read his guilt easily as a poster on a hoarding, watching his dark eyes move helplessly up to the Stafford homestead: the guilt changed slowly into dismay and trapped frustration. He swallowed a congealed spittle but did not speak.

Guilt she could appreciate for her training taught her to discover it, but now she found she could not bear his guiltiness, even against her principles condoning it in pity and wanting to relieve it while seeing clearly all she could ever do or say to this strange, soft, unruly boy was laden with demotic right and proper, well backed by church and state.

Now she had gone so far and was at a loss. She had done what she had intended to do and now pity for his loneliness and anxiousness disarmed her indignation.

She shuddered, for the first time seeing bleakness in his unforgiving and for the first time wanting to see the little plain gray fence she had built around herself to hide a lonely woman from the world because the world had always left the woman lonely.

"My God," she whispered. "My God, what am I to do and what am I thinking . . . ?"

He saw her lips move, her body taut and stiff, his hands by his sides awaiting the next blow and wondering just how far the censure would be carried and how many strangers would be involved, hearing the parish righteousness give tongue, its mouth armed like a pike's mouth with little, cutting, tearing teeth. . . .

Miss Ross was looking directly at him now, not half-past him. His eyes traveled slowly upward from her feet, absently counting seven white bone buttons on her pinafore before they crossed her chin, her neck cords tense with emotion, her mouth, her nose, to rest finally on her slightly protuberant blue eyes that were now damp with tears, her fingers locking her thumbs tightly into her palms.

Without any more profound desire than flight, betraying nothing of the chaos in his mind, he waited much like a ginned animal awaits, mutely without protest for mercy, the final breakneck clout, a small part of his mind idly and nostalgically looking back on all the unsuspected yesterdays, his proud fleet of dreams unburned on this alien shore, and he had moved freely, servant to none.

As if she intuited his will to flight, impulsively she reached out both hands almost as one in deep water would raise his hands in call for help. She held his cheeks between her hands, muttering: "Stephen! Stephen!"

He stood still, quietly admitting her the similar right of parson, parent, bishop, judge or king to scold, chastise and guide. He could smell the faint lavender scent of her clothes and the biting acrid sweat scent of her body and through her soft white hands he felt her trembling. He

looked along her arms at her mouth, the lips drawn off
her teeth a little as slowly and imperceptibly the distance
between them narrowed.

Her face was now close to his, her breath going past
his cheek, their bodies starting to touch and her hands'
position now awkward on his jaws as she tried to bow out
her elbows.

She was sobbing now, strange sobbing almost like
smothered laughter, not making noise with her mouth
but sobbing inside her body, now pressing tightly against
him so he had to brace himself or else be moved back-
ward. Over her shoulder he scanned up and down the
three roads in case someone might appear and think he
was attempting to embrace his teacher; making a meet
with Anne Stafford was bad enough but this on top of
it. . . .

Suddenly she moved, turning swiftly away, her eyes
closed. Surprised, he realized his loins had moved to her
sobbing pressure and he was ashamed, his body's blind
suggestion of a loving with her more distasteful than an
incest.

Dazedly, he watched her pick up the bicycle, still sobbing or laughing, and swing it around hurriedly, her head
turned away from him. Without a word she mounted the
machine and pedaled hard back up the hill, her skirt up
to her knees and billowing out on either side. At the
steep of the brae she stood on the pedals and forced herself along until gravity made her walk. . . .

Slowly he went home and never saw the setting sun
enfire the sky's cirrus. Evening was dusk almost to midnight before he reached his own fields and night was a

maiden queen upon a throne of ebony crystaled by star-shine.

All passion killed, he watched the night, belatedly call-ing her sable name for solace. But somehow he had over-stepped the mark at last and knew the parish ruthlessness for blood would stamp him raper even by intention.

And sleep, long his fond friend, became now a ponder-ous enemy seeking to foil and fox his mind with fog, for-bidding him his schemes of self-defense. He had no case. His mother in the end might understand, but he could not bring himself to confess her the first lust-longing he had ultimately transmuted; that his mind could entertain lust at all would be to her as bad as full physical accom-plishment; and once self-damned or damned by circum-stances, the parish with its Bible and half a thousand ominous texts from Adam to Revelation would never give him any benefit.

The morning came without respite, the first clean, blessed seconds of awaking plunged into the hopeless bowels of his predicament. He cycled slowly to school, stretching the two short miles to leagues: as if already banned, he never saw the beauty of the day that in the night had changed and now was distant gray for rain. Down the last straight stretch he saw the rector's car be-side the school gate, the children milling round it.

"No school, Stephen! No school today!" they greeted him, skipping and dancing in their joy. Fooney Murray danced awkwardly from one foot to the other like a great bear, not knowing why, but dancing all the same. Stephen smiled at Fooney, envying him his untouchable vacuum and willing to swap cleverness for bland idiocy.

The rector nodded without smiling and went on talking to a neighboring farmer whose name was also Stafford, a parish pillar and a brother to Anne's father.

Stephen put his bicycle in the shed, unable any longer to wonder what was in store. He went into the schoolroom, the opening door jeering nemesis with its squeaking groan that yesterday had seemed quaint.

The room was empty save for Anne Stafford. She sat in her accustomed place and did not turn around, her shoulders hunched over the desk.

"Anne?" he whispered. "What's up—tell me?"

She did not reply and he heard the rector coming up the path, and sat on a form along the wall, gauging the distance from seat to door in case the reckoning was past bearing.

The tall clergyman came in and walked slowly up to the head of the room and stalked back and forth. Stephen held tightly to his form, leg muscles braced against floor.

"Ahem," the rector said, stopping to spit a small phlegm into his handkerchief, then blow his nose loudly, dabbing it several times and wiping his mustache to and fro.

"Err . . . Miss Ross," he commenced. "She—she will not be teaching today. That is—she is dead." He looked at Stephen. "I tell you this since you're senior in the school. She—er—she had an accident, Stephen, last night at the Quarry Turn—er—she lost control of her bicycle down the hill. . . ."

Having said all this he blew his nose again and continued: "The school will close for a week. I want you to tell the other children and see they all go home."

He thought for a moment, looking at the floor, bit his lip, nodded with a weak smile and then went out.

Momentarily forgetting his own troubles, Stephen saw the Quarry Turn, its cliff face sloping down to the Salmon Pool; many a time he had stood on the little roadside wall flinging down stones . . . and now Miss Ross dead? Dead . . . this was safe landfall for all his imaginations: no bar now, no charge, no sentence. . . .

Anne had not moved. He ran over to her, seeing her features strained and pallid.

"What's the matter?" he asked. "You never liked Miss Ross—you said so yourself."

His freedom checked again and he caught the girl's shoulder.

"Anne?" he asked loudly. "Who knows, 'sides us?"

"No one," she muttered, shaking her head.

"What's the matter then?" he demanded impatiently.

She answered with a frown and little shudder.

"What's wrong?" he queried more gently.

Still she kept silent. He looked into her face, trying to read her problem for his own mind's peace. Then another fear came to him. He looked around the schoolhouse, seeing the empty high stool by the top wall before the rows of empty desks and hearing the distant question: "What is the Gaelic for bee, Stephen?" The bee and the window and the green ribbons. . . .

He stared at the stool, almost seeing her sitting there, her heels hitched up on the rung. He looked again at the girl, his eyes now softer, confessing that, had he not firstly wanted her to meet him by the cross, Miss Ross now would be calling the roll. . . .

As if she caught his thought Anne sobbed in her throat, her body moving to the sob as Miss Ross's body had moved. . . .

"Why are you crying?" he asked.

She looked up at him, shaking her head then muttering brokenly:

"I—I met her when I was going down to you. She—she told me to go back home. I—I went along the river to the Quarry for I'd told mother I was going to the Tyrrell's for an hour. I was at the pool when she—she screamed an' I saw her tumbling down with the bicycle. She—she didn't fall straight into the pool. Father says it might have saved her. She hit a rock on the side. . . ."

Stephen saw even as clearly as the girl the body and the bicycle turning over and over in the air and heard the wild scream that somehow had started to gather in her lungs when she sobbed against him. He felt more than heard the soft death-crunch like the sound of a sack of corn dropped from a granary loft. . . .

But even all this was driven aside by the wild wind of his regained freedom. He knew now why Anne was crying. She had no guilt at all. She was just scared. . . .

Feeling a little sick in his stomach, he got up, hearing the happy children outside and then Fooney's frantic cry of, "Stephen! Stephen, save me!"

The door complained as he opened it and he knew it would never have to groan for him again. He stood on the steps, the fool's tormentors fleeing when they saw him.

Drawing a deep breath, he looked around, not knowing how or what to feel. While alive or dead the teacher made little difference to his existence, but still nothing would now be quite the same and, like Fooney, he would carry a dead thing in his pocket smelling faintly of lavender and perspiration, her eyes exactly the color of lavender's misty blue; a broken-backed thing with black, thick, bruised blood in his pocket . . . but his river?

He had lost his river? She had taken with her the Annalee, her blood contaminating it and the greater the dilution with water and with time the more powerful its potency. He would never eat a fish from it or bathe in it or let its water wet his boots. . . .

Suddenly he hated the dead woman, her scream scraping past his eardrums like triumphant laughter. She might have let his river be; and not only this sweet stream once habitat of a goddess named Annalee—all streams and rivers the world across; all occupied by a poor goddess, who once had been a teacher in a little school, with small shamed breasts and a pock-marked face who walked with God.

# The Upper Room

I met Kane in a professional gym where I sparred with boxers much smarter than myself for a dollar a round. I needed the money. Kane said there were easier ways and half-sold me a sleeping partnership in a joint he was opening.

Just after Christmas when good will subsided for another twelve months my landlady decided to put my bags on the hungry side of her door. I went down to see Kane and found him refurbishing the joint which was a twenty by ten yard loft over a garage. To reach the foot of the steep narrow stairway, I had to grope my way through parked cars in poor light.

The place had been a speakeasy before, and its door wore slyly a Judas hole. It gave me the jeebies and never was I able to see it save as I first saw it, shrouded with cobwebs, the justly forgotten tomb of lousy expectations.

Kane took me to his hotel and stood me a good dinner on the slate, and from what I could gather, this slate was already full. Too busy scheming about the money he was going to make, Kane had no time to think about the money he owed.

And that first night in the hotel it was annoying repeatedly to have the bedclothes snatched away. But I was kept awake to witness the man's near-neurotic fear, his face puckered and his powerful body shrinking from some dark pain. Thereafter I knew two Kanes; one inspired dislike but the other prayed pity, and I served the second one in spite of or because of the first.

We opened on a Saturday, and as most of the drinks were on the house, we did not break even. I managed to borrow fifty dollars from a compatriot to keep us going. We had to vacate the hotel via the fire escape and slept for a night in the muslin love nest, an alcove Kane fitted in the joint for any client who desired more privacy for one thing or another.

I voted for staying there awhile cheaply but Kane liked his comforts and found a girl friend's flatlet when the owner was out of town. I got myself a two-dollar attic room which was cold enough to freeze any of my nightmares in their tracks.

By February's end I knew we were getting nowhere and kept looking for a normal job. Kane cheerfully assured me business would mend, and in face of such optimism, pessimism seemed downright indecent.

He was a big good-looking guy about twenty-seven, mouse-brown in coloring, and a topaz fleck in his brown eyes. He said he was the son of a Ukrainian barmaid and an Irish laborer. His full name was Ivan Parnell Kane. His friends called him Nell.

He was not a pansy although he had a few wealthy boy friends on a loose line. They liked to look at him. Many

women, married and single, fell for him and with all his
admirers he was cool and cavalier.

It was an open secret he never used normally any
woman with whom he might from time to time cohabit.
At bar gatherings jokes were made about his erotic pro-
clivities and the pansies reverentially respected him much
as a Chinese respects a woman for her tiny feet. They de-
lighted in a catchpenny game to do with the size of a
man's hand in relation to the phallus. Kane had huge
hands.

At a penthouse spree he met a girl and she tumbled
for him. This was around the first week in March. She
was wealthy enough in those dour times to own a hack and
ride it in the park; no more than a blonde kid with small
hard proud nodules for breasts, slim body and an attractive gait, and in a spoiled way surly pretty.

Almost every evening she came to the joint, spending
money on drinks and gazing at Nell. He got fed up with
the lark of having to take her home, tipsy and full of un-
requited love, even if she did pay for the taxi both ways.

I figured that an average man might or might not take
this girl for one of many reasons, but Kane was not average. He was amoral and his reluctance ran counter to his
bar philosophy. I could not understand it. He could have
married, lived with, or sponged on her.

Helen was her name and eventually the joint proved to
be her sordid Troy minus Kane as Menelaus or Paris, or
any other bottle-hero who might fancy her between drinks
as she sat silent, sullen by her love. I never talked to her. I
was too shy, the very virulence of her affliction holding me

away. I might even have loved her, for she was clean and charming, but did not desire her in loyalty to Kane.

Like any other job, my life had a rhythm: I worked till dawn, slept to eleven, and usually wandered about the town looking at people and things and spending the wet cold hours in museums in which I learned a great deal about America and the world.

Easter was the last week in March that year and Kane was preparing to celebrate it, if not with wine and wafer, with gin and ginger ale.

When walking along Park Avenue north of the Grand Central—my favorite street—I witnessed spring storming the winter-weary city that since Christmas had been gray and sleet and frost.

Quite suddenly the sun was kindly warm again and lightsome, and it was as if I had been groping along a dark cold tunnel where twilit people moved and muttered beyond the changing beauty of the nights.

And now I had come forth, gloom-blinded, unsure, but still whole and glad into sunlight. Standing, I gazed around, wanting to take off my hat and let the sun's great light shine on my head; to lift my arms, holding up in my hands my poor life, to shout my news and tell the sun still lived, that it was good, that it made mosaic of gold the stony pavement, that by its light I could see again the plains and the rivers, the forests and high mountains rising to the sky like frozen prayers.

After that the joint was a tawdry place. I came in about five. The equestrienne was already there and unromantically Kane himself was cleaning up and getting ready for a big night.

He was surly and had been so for some days. The girl who owned the flat he occupied had returned early and while not wanting to throw him out, she apparently expected some return in kind if not in cash.

The possibility of having to vacate free and comfortable rooms upset him so much that the night before he had been his own best customer and in answer to my suggestion that a working compromise should not be impossible he had hinted at some early trouble with thugs in Chicago when he was only eighteen.

Rubber-legged and flabby I got him home. His attractive landlady was in bed. Since he expected to be sick I left him sitting safely on the toilet seat, his girl friend nursing what she took to be his indifference.

And now Helen nursed a similar idea as she sat at a table sipping a drink. She was dressed in jodhpurs, having come straight from the Park, hitching her horse in the garage below.

I watched them and figured I knew my Kane now, not as enemy or rival nor as a Demetrius to his unlettered Origen: as a brother. He was devoid of any of love's faculties; an unscrupulous Narses but lacking a Narses' skill.

His admirers gave him credit for what they did not have themselves—a touch, perhaps, of Wordsworth's immortality and a pagan unshriven sanctity beyond law's form, content and compression: all his suitors sick spoiled pagans in their hearts, escapers all from their own wildernesses and seeking Kane a desert John to make their barrenness flower again.

# 2

On top of spring and everything I was feeling odd and had hated to climb the stairs. In any allegory on hell one usually steps down a winding stair but I had climbed this flight of dusty steps, each step alive with dismal groan, to reach a minor limbo scented with stale smoke and booze: and Kane was a jailer when he let me in.

I felt nothing remotely personal against the man; he was my elder brother and in my youth I needed him for guide and patron in this his vicious and uncaring realm. My past did not deny our brotherhood. I was no saint. What did deny it was my life, that whole part of my life as yet unlived, the timeless and errorless part as yet unborn which the unspent days, were I careful, would bear cleanly and lawfully without taint of abortion. Loudly my un-lived life said no to him and no to his life attitude and no to our occupation and no to all such useless usury.

This was not my America, this hole-and-corner cop-bribing end of the sewer existence; this braggadocio, this cave of bum-boys, tarts, small crooks. I could have found similar not ten miles from my home under the hills with-out the trouble of traveling abroad at all . . . no.

No: not my continent which was an undying persistent dream denied at times by the land's very citizens; a dream of far distances and spating starshine, rivers leaping to their oceans, avalanche, slow glacier, and sun-hot rock. . . .

Watching shirt-sleeved Kane polishing glasses and con-

scious of this love-tormented girl who metaphorically lay
wide-legged on the floor for him, I wanted to weep because
I knew too that Kane had schemes if not dreams; his Helen
and any other Kane or Helen had their dreams concerned
with circumstances potential or impossible; better smaller
dreams than mine and far more important than any lofty
pine combing gently the moonlight through her hair:
my own impediment—a veined leaf more valid in my sight
than veined human hand.

Kane was saying he had hired a tame musician, and at
seven this man arrived, a slight pale chap about thirty
named Larry. He smiled and said howdy, an unlit cigarette drooping from the corner of his thin-lipped mouth,
his hat on the back of his head. He accepted a drink, made
himself comfortable at the piano and started gently, ex-
ploringly to play.

He was a jazz dope; his wife was any piano and he
caressed her with limp fingers and played gooey or hot
love songs on her body, his down-at-heels beating out the
rhythm like a witch doctor's tom-tom: a heart's sub-beat
to do with fornications in a jungle.

Soon as the music started I felt even more strange and
began to worry because on the three occasions I had felt
like this someone closely connected with me had died suddenly. And I did not need death for I had life, and life
was sweet again with spring.

Kane admitted the two unemployed chorus girls. They
were not prostitutes but had to stay alive. Gracie the big
blonde was an open charming girl from the Middle West
with a hunted look in her eyes because she knew time and

depression were dating her. I could never get near her. She knew I had no money, and were I more than time-of-day talkative she would suspect I was after a free insertion although she was nowhere near my personal sexual pick. Big women like that embarrassed me.

Kane said he had slept with her, boasting to his barflies how he had used her, and on the evening after the rendez-vous they gave her a stone-throwing fox-scorning cheer.

She took the salutation, not hating them because her reputation was soiled but because her generic decency was offended, the intimacy, be what it was, now a telephone pole against which they cocked their legs.

The second girl the wits named Disgracie. She was small, dark, and suspicious, with a singing voice like a bagpipes; strong-bodied and a sort of acrobat by profession, and while not so pretty as the blonde the men preferred her since they said her stage technique could be adapted to the world that was a bed.

I was behind the bar and stood the girls a drink. They were hungry, for they started on the pretzels. I saw them glancing at the horsewoman with equal envy and scorn.

A gauche, untutored male, I watched them climb gingerly into the echoing suffering house of Helen's soul, whispering comments to each other as they crept through the rooms in which Kane's name and personality moved, an echo's ghost, every room a love nest but empty of anything to love. It made me sort of ill to see such feline clinical unpity.

And tipsy-dull as Helen was, the female grapevine gossiped its spiteful news. She pulled herself together, arose

and went to the toilet to issue forth again well made-up
and soignée even in jodhpurs and hacking jacket. And in
spite of her misery, she made her point.

We waited for cash customers. Kane put on his jacket
and stuck out his chest, talking about grands. I listened
and could not help thinking how recently he had started
to swing me on the till.

This I accepted; he made the contacts and was worth
more. For the sake of sounder bookkeeping I had tried to
arrange a two-way split after putting by a percentage
against rent, cop rent, and booze. But he would not admit
any dissatisfaction, much less the implication of double-
dealing.

One of his more constant boy friends wandered in and
bought us all a drink. I followed the barkeep's law and
drank for gin a straight of ginger ale. This was a quiet
gray-haired man, and I saw nothing odd about him, but
I had no understanding at all for this facet of love.

It was Kane's birthday and the man had brought along
a present—a set of gold links and studs. Kane accepted the
gift and then took the man over to Helen, introduced
them, left them together, and thereafter ignored them.

The joint was filling up. Customers sat at tables or
stood in clumps or lounged against the bar. It was too
early yet for noise and released inhibitions. All seemed
set fair for a busy Saturday night and tomorrow, Sunday,
was rent day: better the day, better the rent.

I was trying to focus and rationally to observe what
went on around me and inside me, and it was difficult to
work while matching the two moving plates which insisted on contesting vision. If I closed my eyes one plate

remained and was like a dream which frightened me as Kane was frightened when asleep; as I had been frightened when a child, waking up with swimming myopic sight and trembling hands that reached the far distance to a table or a chair for comfort and reality; as all who have been children know these things and know their power and terror: the solid, solid earth soft and way-giving; not insecure so much as unpredictable.

I thought if I had a strong drink I'd feel better. I made one but couldn't drink it, and if I had it would have hit my stomach and then bounced back again. I feared I was getting ill—not that being ill worried me but being ill when broke and without home, friends, or help. . . .

I tried to tell myself I was strong; I was tough as big man Kane and had at times worked through utter weariness into strength again, which few of these people had ever done. . . .

# 3

Then there came loud poundings from the stairs. Everyone went tense and swiftly Kane slipped to his Judas hole, returning with a reassuring smile. Seeing the smile the customers relaxed. The scufflings on the stairs increased and Kane opened the door to admit several breathless jokers and a horse.

It was an odd sight indeed to see a full-grown hunter coming into a crowded speak; one woman screamed, hiding her face in her escort's shoulder, and a drunk said *fatally:* What d'ye know? Guess I've seen about everythin' now.

Kane led the animal into the middle of the room and they made a ring around it with tables, admiring and half sorry and not quite sure if the prank were tasty or not.

The horse seemed easy enough. It moved to a table and knocked a highball into a girl's lap and cleaned up a little dish of peanuts with its big loose lips, chewing and slobbering and looking craftily around as if pub-crawls were normal as eating hay at home.

A pot-valiant wanting to share his elation with the brute creation insisted on giving the horse a drink and ordered five dollars' worth of highballs. I tried to suggest that such a stoup might be too much at once, even for a horse, but seriously he answered with the formula that the animal was ten times larger than he was and one drink had never done him any harm. Obviously thirsty, the horse whinnied when it saw the liquid slopping in the bowl and the drunk said: What did I tell you? It drank up every drop and looked for more. The drunk patted it, saying it was a horse after his own heart, but he did not spend another fivespot. I refilled the bowl with water for a chaser.

In a very short time the great inoffensive beast was accepted and people seemed to forget it was a horse, fresh clients getting a shock and raising a laugh when they reacted to it.

They noticed Helen's suitable attire and called on her for a riding demonstration, and unable finally to withstand any more harmless banter which her misery barbed, she arose and came to the bar, scribbled a little note for Kane and then walked out, followed by horse-calls.

I felt in my stomach her deep hurt. All knew of her complaint, Juan Kane made no secret of it, preening himself because this Four Hundred's daughter named his big feet golden as a god's.

Trade was now brisk, and I could not stop even to think until with a definite snap I split into two and watched the hands of my body fill glasses and change money, my body itself almost another stranger.

I saw everything quite clearly and normally and I could hear and see Larry's playing, stuff like gray treacle flowing slowly out of the piano and unto the floor, people walking through it.

But this clarity did not last, becoming confused again, and I knew with nervousness that if there was a second snap I might be dead. I did not think this. I knew. And out of the shrouded empty love nest there were issuing forms and people who slipped like ghosts among the clients, moving around and through them in a dimension that was not human.

The room became thronged with these brown-purple uninvited guests, space and time now seeming fused in one dimension in which I also seemed to exist; not unnaturally as if this fusion was a constant factor and I had not been aware of it.

As I made thoughts vague forms went out from me and joined the others. It was some time before I realized that these forms were my own thoughts or half-thoughts no longer framed in word or concept such as I normally and naively thought thinking to be: light and freely living things, the brain pressing them out of its own substance much as a linotype imprints its symbols on molten lead.

I was not unhappy until I realized I was not, and this led to a self-consciousness which brought a great sense of insecurity and this in turn disturbed all the forms before me, moiling them into a haze of indistinct movement in which no single one was visible.

Not yet appreciating the formative power in my thinking, I thought that I had been existing like a bat, and a bat form appeared from me, perfectly bat-shaped, the slowly pulsing wings suspending the body as if it bobbed on a string, right before my eyes.

This bat scared me. I could not close my eyes against it because this sight I possessed lacked lids to avoid either ugliness or beauty. I had to face the bat: and now there were other bats, flying about and most batlike as if the joint were a bat roost and they were out to taste the night. My own specimen did not join these others and I had to stare through its horribly half-human devilish face with fangs that curled its upper lip into a snarl, its pug nose like a pig's.

So I could cling to the tatters of my consciousness, I tried to see the human reality before me and give it a time-name so I might also name myself in time and not mad; but curving inwards, my thoughts saw my own head —a snakepit, snake foul and whispering with sibilant snake rustle of dry scales, a sound no other animal may make: my own head Medusa. . . .

I knew the clients were making much of their dull horse, time's ancient symbol for intelligence swifter than any arrow flighting to its kill: Troy, Helen, and Hector old Priam's heir; Kane Ulysses to my foreboding Achilles; or else a helpless Perseus seeking the Pegasus of true intelligence that had little to do with body-want, pleasure, or love of ease.

The customers were raking through myth, fable, poetry and legend in search of a horse's name, the exercise prolonged because it gave some the opportunity to parade erudition. Kane looked wise when old great names were mentioned as if he knew not only the name's sound but also him who wore it: Ha, Venus! Howya Remus. . . .

Bellerophon? No, not I, by god, although I could well claim old Sisyphus for ancestor as could we all, pushing our boulders up the endless hill and taking almost with gladness the brutal blow when they returned, seeking an unconsciousness if not a death: death we could not have—deathless are those who exist in hell.

Abelard was the name elected, chiefly because the horse was a gelding. All round it fitted nicely for me: Kane, Kane's Helen, Heloise, and Heloise could not have Kane or Abelard . . . but Helen-Heloise? I hoped she had found her own warm bed, lonely as it might be, and did not seek solace in the cold corridors of Abbess Hudson's nunnery. . . .

I remembered her little note and gave it to Kane. He read it and chucked it back to me: *Dear Nell, I'm sorry I forgot your birthday. You never said: Please have the horse as a present. Helen.*

Paul R. Kane took the note and rode around the gin party with a flourish, spreading the news. Soon all began to sing happy birthday dear Nellie happy birthday to you. Larry slipped easily into the melody and made much of it after the three weak cheers.

Bathed in this shallow pool of fame, Kane called the

house for drinks which the house could ill afford. They all crowded around the bar, several men hoisting Kane up on it, someone leading Abelard over.

They lifted their glasses in a toast and it was as if we all worshiped a dull and drunken horse, its magic dead; toasting it in poor libidinous bacchanal in hope that its emasculated intelligence might give us reason for life again. . . .

I was seeing now, not the joint, but a forgotten temple, the walls covered not with meditative mural but with masturbative nudes that moved and lived, squirming their hips and jerking forward their genitals to inspire active eroticism instead of prayer.

In spite of Larry's left-hand beat that timed the whole procedure I tried to get away from bats and make my mind see that other love act that moved serenely in simple splendor with its seven unresentful passions and seven times seven times seven restraint. . . .

But I could not hold it and saw instead a bald potbellied Pilate peering through his Judas hole, Herod biting his nails and asking if it were over, and Peter smoking fag ends and hanging round the stairs, scared to talk in case the temple toughs hoisted him by his scrotum.

But they were all there—all waiting for the end: Joseph who sailed they say to England, Jew wandering or Jew at home, Roman, Greek, Babylonian, Frank, wild men from forest-silent Germany, and secret slant-eyed children off the steppes; Celt, Egyptian, Persian, Indian, coal-black strong men from Nubia and beyond, Chinese merchants with great caravans of rich brocades, and furred horsemen from far Thule . . . come one and all! Happy deathday to you!

To break my thrall I clawed at a memory of home: daffodils and the last of the snowdrops, golden chimes instead of frozen tears: Mary's tears my mother said, carried by heaven's four winds over all the earth to break at the year's matins the cold sod and bravely weep: do not carry them into the house, she said, it is not lucky; tears on the hearth of home; do not take them off the earth, let it weep silently. . . .

I knew that this vernal point in the world's spiral had a holiness, whether from God Himself or hallow d by the continual rites of men . . . no matter: pagan and Christian pressing their ceremony into the earth's life-memory, and could stone speak or mineral cry as tin they would declare Easter by some forgotten name or rune. . . .

# 4

A little rough drunk decided Abelard should be christened and clambered up on a table to do the job with a highball. At that moment Abelard lay down, heaving out its great chest and knocking drunk and table over. It sighed and went to sleep and the drunk stunned himself on the floor.

Already the news had gone about we had a horse in the joint and people were coming up to see it. Abelard lay on its side, its rump blocking the toilet door. No hard-pressed female could slip into the toilet without having to straddle the horse's hams, and this gave wits the opportunity to scrawl graffiti on the very air through which danced naked female bottoms chased by rampant phalli, and all the gray-brown forms grew fat, feeding on the lubricity.

Some customers started to worry about Abelard's health and buttonholed Kane who said I was an expert on horse-flesh and called me in to lull the oversensitive sympathies. Abelard was all right.

My knowledge impressed the little drunk so much that he insisted I drink with him. I could hardly see him. He seemed grotesque and at times huge much as I suspect a stoat appears to a rabbit. He had a big man's torso and a small man's legs and his hands were large and softly white with broad blunt wedges for thumbs. Terror moved about his small dried head.

His nearness made me ill. He discovered I was Irish and made me his first dyed-in-the-bog Irishman, stroking me and admiring me, saying his grandparents on both sides had been Irish and making me talk so he could taste my brogue.

Calling over his girl friend, he related with joy what a grand Irish kid I was, making me do my stuff all over again. Had he asked me to stand on my head and sing the sweet shamrock I would have complied because my will, like my body, was limp as a coach leather and it didn't matter what he said or what I did.

My Irishness did not move the girl. She threw her big pale-blue-mascaraed eyes over me and agreed, saying non-committally: Yea, Joe. Sure, Joe. . . .

She made me think of silver eels and water-shining things, of chill mermaids loving drowned mariners and wailing in their water rut, their mating cold as salmon sperming eggs in sand; moon pools in tidal rocks, her bones coral and eyes sea-green pearls; shark snap and tide rip and sibilant silken laughter. . . .

Spiders . . . no, I denied, forcing the thought away.

This empty blonde, how she might live and how die I did not know; this Arachne, this spider queen, close-spinning love that ended in a devouring: her forearms had a soft pappus of white hair, setae and light-touch sensitive to slightest movement on her passion's net; and on her brink she would become all spideress, neither pain nor pleasure sharing her ecstasy, tasting death's very sweetness with silent wide-mouthed scream for more and more through every fiber of her webbed body. . . .

Joe was saying the girl was a Swede, Helda by name, and next to the Irish the Swedes were okay. Helda did not listen and spent her time eyeing the other women critically and impersonally. Sideways, her face was lovely as a flower and soulless as a flower.

Joe's arm was tightening round my shoulders and he whispered confidentially as he lifted his coat away to reveal a holster full of black automatic: Don't forget, kid? If any sonofabitch insults ya—let me know! Let Joe Nolan know?

No. . . . Nolan no know . . . no sonofabitch know Nolan. A man hovered above his head, the face of it warped in agony and the hands grasping tightly at its belly as if to pull forth pain and slugs and death. . . .

Helda glanced at me curiously as sweat dropped through my eyebrows off my forehead. Joe himself did not worry me—men kill and men sleep, love, feed, lust, and gamble with life as if it were a race between two wind-blown straws on a common. But no Nolan: I had seen a knife in a man's back—but not for money; I'd seen a Negro's guts fall down around his feet like gray moving worms—but not for cold money . . . no, no, Nolan.

There was a sudden loud single knock on the door. It should have been a one-two-one. Kane looked up and moved away from the bar, slipping on his hat and overcoat. The clients read his actions and went silent. Larry played on.

Nolan changed. His eyes no longer swam in Hibernian seas. They were round and crafty-cold. Helda laid her hand on the table, palm uppermost, and Joe drew his gun and laid it on her palm.

With her left hand as she withdrew the right one, she lifted her skirt. She had long slim thighs, frost-pale and blue as skim milk, and I felt the numbness that was my body surge into life and reach out to her because her thighs were so cold they should burn as frozen iron, viciously and without first hurt or warning.

She wore black net briefs that were tight on her as a jock strap, the strange ferret fur of her thickening and darkening in two manes along the palms of her thighs to her crotch.

Swiftly she plucked the elastic top away from her midriff that was flat and hard as a boy's and tucked the gun down one leg so it lay on the inside of a thigh. I heard the elastic snap back against her skin as she took the holster Joe had unharnessed and stuffed it into her handbag. All this happened in the time it took Kane to walk twelve paces to the door.

He peered through the Judas port, talking and asking questions, then gave the customers an okay as he drew the bolts. Two men walked in. One was small, slim, and natty in a blue pin-stripe suit and the other was twice his escort's size and soberly attired in dark gray like a bishop in mufti.

Kane glanced at me as he passed. He did not like these strangers. Their effect on Joe Nolan was such that he nodded to Helda, and they arose and did not even bid me good-by as I let them out.

The strangers invited the chorus girls to drink and Kane served them while I gathered a tray of empty glasses. Kane washed a few glasses and left me for the floor, taking off hat and coat again.

Both strangers carried guns. The bishop betrayed his colossal vanity only by wearing a ring-watch on the hook of a little finger. He had a habit of toying with the lobe of his left ear with a forefinger. A spider was sitting inside the ear and forever tickling him.

He sipped his drink, tasting it carefully, and casually undressed the blonde. Without any stirring of his passion he examined her, finding another tolerable nude with large breasts that no longer had the impertinent lift of youth. He found little to interest him and almost he shook his head. There was no female in the joint fit to stir him. He had long since passed garden fornication and wanted terror in his love such as a young unbroken girl might give him. The blonde turned around to give him a better view, night was wearing thin and her friandise decreased with the pace of the dawn's approach.

Some customers had cleared a ten-foot square before the bar and had started a dance. The little stranger asked Disgracie to dance. They slid around, the man's hand pressing hard on the small of the girl's back so that her pelvis pressed into his loins, his thigh sliding between her thighs and lingering there on the slow exaggerated turns.

# 5

Like a shoal of leaves wind-swirled into a corner there was a sudden influx of half a dozen unemployed chorus boys who hunted in a pack from the Village to Harlem. I never discovered how or where they lived or what they ate for solid food. They moved by night and I never saw them by the sun. They all had pale, puffy, smooth-shaven talc-whitened faces like plants forced in darkness; six boys— one face. But they were not dislikable, and were always full of a ruthless goading gaiety all their own.

And yet they knew nothing of the night where stars still flung a sequined gauntlet into the rocky-hearted streets and valleys of their city. And my mother was simple-minded when she whispered night was a thing, an entity, with sad dark eyes in a pallid-purple face, indwelling in shadow and lying daylong in caves where sun's fingers could never reach, waiting for evenset and flight of bat her leathern dove that said with cypress branch the sun had gone: and sometimes she listened with a forlorn smile to song of nightingale her only sweetly faithful bird; or else she ground her toothless gums with anile rage, storming and scratching with cruel nails the windowpane or tearing ivy off the walls, all wet with rain that was her copious and unending tears. . . .

But the boys were in high fettle. They had found a

sugar-matron. She leapt from the toilet across Abelard like a roe. All half dozen crowded under her molted wing, chickens too tough for any lesser wing than Gabriel's.

She planked a tenspot on the bar and told me with a wink to holler when it was spent and then put new life into Larry by paying for five dollars' worth of music.

Not yet believing in the pack's luck, one of her gallants told me they had found her chafing in a staid hotel. She had come to town to play from some hick hamlet where they still used hitching rails instead of car parks. Alive, her husband had been strict and parsimonious; dead, he had left her his fortune and she was Jerusalem-bent to catch up on her wasted years.

For me, a Medusa with snakes in her public hair; haggard and harmless and probably over sixty. Her make-up was daubed on as if she had done it in a hurry in the dark. The customers could not take her seriously although her boy friend boasted she took all six to bed with her. A few of the clients were offended and one said loudly that her ass should be kicked. Had the grandam been forty years younger this guy would not have wanted to kick her.

Almost with unbelief I realized that when this woman was a girl, America had still been young, the Civil War a living memory; buggies, badlands, and buckaroos.

Sensing the bishop's fatherly indifference, and not wanting to appear too easy, Gracie had wandered over to the piano and gave the joint a song in her pleasing husky voice. She sang about tomatoes being cheaper, bananas cheaper . . . and Larry played that bums, bottoms, hymens, and all male and female appurtenances were cheaper and being so time was love-ripe bom-bom, bom-bom, bom. . . .

We ran short of ginger ale and I had to go down to the all-night drugstore which supplied us at a cut rate. Larry's bom-bom followed me down the stairs where a queue of gray zombies waited to come in, all pulsing to the piano's mesmeric beat.

I shut my eyes, letting my feet feel for the steps, and ran down into the lofty cool garage that reeked with the mixed spices of gasoline, leather, paint, old perfume. . . .

In the still gloom the cars slept, prehistoric beasts. I had now a world bedded forever in iron, ice, and rock; an underworld, sleep-silent and undead. And Larry's bom-bom was a knotted line paying out faintly from above, connecting me with the living dead. . . .

Breathing deeply the cleaner air outside I felt better, objects coming back with steadier focus, and the dingy street of joints, cheap hotels, and garages seemed quite beautiful, the darkness hiding the ash-can commonness.

Just above the roofs at arm's length swung stars at anchor in a sky made opalescent by the waning three-quarter moon. When I reached the corner a bright planet was hovering in the west and Orion's bull with lowered head sniffed at Times Square.

The great square was empty and odd in the night; world-famous as it was, it also had its night and was inhabited only by one strolling cop, a few bums, and a rabble of revelers outside an all-night chophouse, a male voice calling arrogantly for a taxi and taxi taxi taxi chased the frail echo of a tipsy female's extravagant laughter.

I did not want to buy ginger ale or to return to the speak. Two things made me go back: one was the helpless Abelard; the other was a gambler's faith in a winning run so I could repay the fifty-dollar loan—money for which my compatriot had worked hard and honestly.

Gracie was still singing and going down well with the trade. She had no boy friend and no money and impulsively I took Abelard's bowl and set it on a table, dropping a half dollar into it, and gradually everyone followed suit, each one ashamed not to donate.

Leaves falling . . . Gracie was singing now; leaves tumbling down, she said, obeying the lyric but not knowing it was spring now and leaves were puckered powerful things straining against the shell of their sheath and longing for the sun. . . .

The dancing went on, the tireless grandam using her team like batons in a relay; the acrobat and the bishop's acolyte sliding over the floor, close as two mating snails.

A drunk temporally upset the rhythm by buying Larry a drink and insisting it was Christmas and not Easter and Larry obliged with the Venite until Kane checked him in case the clients disliked carousal in a church, and the bishop frowned heavily at the breach of good taste.

The hymn pressed back the festival theme into my mind but instead of any religious image I saw the joint as first I had seen it and now the spiders were returning.

They crawled everywhere and this bishop was the archspider, gray and fat on flesh with death-wise eyes of lead under tufted brows that were his setae. And he had art enough to move lightly on the sticky web stretched over the bars of the corroded law and spun for him by us all, for we were lesser spiders hiding in the grass of our greed with spinning wheels in our backsides which twisted ropes of shitsilk to trap the petty victims of our lusts. . . .

Maybe I was shouting and everyone was listening to me. I do not know. I only saw the spiders eating what I said or thought and excreting strands of mock gossamer.

I said we were not blind, not night-blind, for bats can see-feel a cotton thread at night and our own spunshit threads echoed unerringly to a quarry's touch.

The spiders moved into a circle around the bishop and it seemed the customers were there too—all but Larry who played faithfully to his wife and spun a master web of rhythm.

I saw no pity in the spiders' eyes, for myself or for themselves; each one was the other's inevitable enemy, speed to escape and strength to destroy their only assets.

Yes, I could assent, mea culpa, mea culpa. Good bishop. . . .

What is life? the bishop-spider asked.

It's neither large nor small, I tried to say, not wishing to appear clever. It's neither hard nor easy and it's only so seen in any man's personal dimension which is not accurate and is but a prejudiced estimation which depends on many little things like a bellyache or a gumboil.

Blasphemy, the bishop said.

No, I denied, scared that indeed I might be blashphemous, saying things that might well be true but also antisocial. I love life, I protested. I wouldn't hurt that which I love?

Man hates the things he loves, the bishop muttered, stating an inevitable law. Love is passive and negative. Hate is active and positive.

If not love then, pity? I pleaded. It is not womanish to pity? Pity is a full man's possession and women have none.

They have a cancerous compassion which is not truly of earth at all and is in reality an angelic phenomenon to do with all mankind and not with the differentiated man. Gods stoop not as far as pity, they have compassion as women have did they not stoop to self-pity. . . .

Words—mere words, the bishop said, feeding his spiders on them.

With a tightly closed fist he made a pass in the air and said: Confess.

I saw then the joint's true figurehead still-carved in pruinose alabaster . . . Joe Nolan's Helda.

Contentedly she stood naked within her silkshit house, not asking for lover's poem nor tomcat's serenade, couch stripped for action like a battle deck. I hung my head, saying:

Mea culpa . . . this lean hag, this gunman's charwoman, this female illusion of youth; this witch empowered to wind her arms around me, drawing forth my life and storing my semen in a jam jar. . . .

I take this Helda, this icicle of frozen slops who is clean when cold but only a dirty puddle when she melts, this cold hot coal, this moon-moll, this mobster's mistress in the moon . . . mea culpa.

Take her, the bishop said, listening to me as if I were telling a dirty joke.

. . . and cunningly distill, I repeated as if after him, the precious acrid drops of passion and when distilled, refine them down to the volatile oil essential of pure lust. Do not enchild her and make her heavy-laden with sentiment! Keep her lean and hungry-sharp! Bait her to make her wicked! Bedevil her so that she never trusts in anything but the down-delving dark deep drive of passion! And then die into her body. . . .

The fat white hands were shredding my thoughts as they came to him and feeding them to his spiders as crumbs to birds. He lifted his tired gray eyes to my face, asking if I had more to say, his spiders now waiting by my lips.

I knew I was not mad nor going mad: we were all sub-mad as animals are fully sub-mad; my sanity matched with higher or lower norm might well be madness, sanity itself but relative to any state of life; true madness a healthy ecstasy as saints and poets have it. . . .

The spiders' nearness revolted me and to drive them back I tried to reach for any image which might not be palatable to them. I saw a sloping plain of rock under a rising swelling moon and a stream—a stream caught in a gray rock-vise for her to burnish so she might know her own great beauty. . . .

Slowly the spiders crept away, unable to devour these thoughts, and I saw the bishop toying with his ring-watch, seeing and hearing nothing.

# 6

Medusa, not content with keeping six males moving, tried to rake others into the dance and boned the bishop, catching his coat with an irreverent hand. Horrified, the acolyte dropped Disgracie and shoved the old woman away just as his righteous reverence was about to swing a heavy hand across her mouth.

I watched the acolyte brush the bishop down, my stomach turning over. I did not know what I would have done had he thus roughly laid hands on my Medusa.

Nonplused, she marshaled her six pimps into a semblance of a square dance, instructing Larry to play a suitable air. Disregarding her directions which she began solemnly to intone, the boys made a game for themselves.

Their movements were the dance of the mating spiders; they waved their legs, arms, and bodies like sexual palpi in an obscene mime halfway between male and female: or else they danced as six satyrs, nimble as chamois and lecherous as billy goats, keeping themselves at concitement's pitch by smelling their own genitals.

But dirty as it was it raised laughter because it was also original and funny with Medusa moving through her square dance and yowling at the corners, quite unaware.

The bishop remained aloof but when one of the boys stood at the piano in an excess of entertainment and accompanied the mimeodrama in a high tenor with a pornographic parody of Under the Old Apple Tree, the bishop refused to stand it any longer, and backed by ecumenical authority he stalked over and smacked the singer heavily across the face while the protective acolyte watched approvingly, a fag drooping from his lips, his head on one side, and his hands hanging loose. I suppose the bishop was really a pure man at heart. After that, Medusa and her rout packed up and fled.

Pontifically, the bishop ordered four more drinks and paid for them with a fivespot. When I gave him the three dollars' change he challenged me quietly, claiming he had given me ten bucks. In a whisper I denied this, staring at

him, something telling me not to argue. Minus his gun
and animated gun-hod I could have slapped this big bastard happily round the block. The acolyte forestalled any
trouble by saying with a large wink:

Okay. Okay. This joint's okay.

The bishop shrugged and took no further interest, I
knew now who he was. I thought Kane had been wolf-
wolfing about him just to be big. We were in his diocese
and he expected us to pay tithe. . . .

Abelard relieved some of the tension by standing up,
yawning, and spending all of two dollars on the threshold
of the toilet door. The customers rewarded it with pretzels
while Kane cleaned up the mess, saying it was for his
pansies when asked what he intended to do with it.

But I knew now something was going to happen and
someone was going to get hurt and that it could be Kane,
for a gray shadow sat on his shoulder. My sweat started to
prickle as if I were under a jet of steam. I tried to catch
Kane's eye but he had forgotten me save as a barhop and
anything I might say would make no difference.

Larry's piano was sounding right inside my chest and
all the room's shadows mimed and danced with threat in
every swirl and the night hastened to its dawn.

I could not withstand another spider session and tried
to find thoughts that would keep them away: Easter's
dawn, I thought, and the wonder of the Resurrection; this
very morning in a gray dawn, a crowded city hushed in
guilt and people tossing on their beds and dreaming anxiously of the cry that had raced around the world. . . . Eli
Eli lama. . . .

This very dawn one thousand eight hundred and ninety-nine years before stout soldiers had had the wits scared out of them, the terrible cry returning from farthest nebula as an echo to its site: Eli Eli. . . .

That cleared the room of spiders and suddenly the acrobat hit her acolyte across the mouth. With the chest-high bar between us I could not see what he had done. Disgracie had never previously objected to a hand on her knee.

The acolyte did not even stiffen. I thought he was going to pass it. He leaned loosely on the bar, his right arm lying on it. He did not move until he drove a right hook unto the girl's jaw, pivoting away with the blow. She dropped out of my sight and no one would have noticed anything had Kane not stepped in.

I suppose it was the Kane asleep who acted, for Kane awake had no great motive. He steamed over and caught the acolyte by the coat, hitting him a chopping right.

The little man dropped, then reappeared clawing at Kane's legs. Kane tried to kick him away but was brought down and Larry still accompanied and everything rushed past me and the gray smoke-filled zombies swirled among the customers who were slowly waking up to the fact that a roughhouse was rounding off their night. Had I felt pain then I would have been in agony; a similar pain to that which a man feels in the crushed hand belonging to the arm which has been amputated.

The bishop kept calm but slipped his hand under his jacket and Gracie grabbed a bottle and hit him smartly on the head, then she took his gun and threw it behind the bar.

The acolyte could not have known that Kane sometimes earned an honest if too strenuous dollar by sparring with all-in wrestlers, and that was his mistake. Kane lugged him to his feet, hit him twice and let him go. That was Kane's error.

The little man staggered back, trying to save himself from falling, and just missing Abelard. He backed to the end wall, clutching the love nest's muslin curtains and pulling them down around him so he looked like an ecstatic celebrant all ready for a sacrifice.

Go in! I shouted to Kane but instead he crouched and put on a Garden act for the clients. I was right behind him and the acolyte was trying to draw his gun, his hand wrapped up in a web of cheesecloth. His eyes were round and staring and I knew he did not see humans any more, no more than a bull sees anything at the exact moment of truth.

There was a sheet of ply between me and three-eight slugs and old Larry was strumming away like flowers in June inside my head with his bom-bom, bom-bom, bom and the little gray man on Kane's neck was riding like a jockey.

The customers were pressed against the safest wall and Abelard looked around, half puzzled by the sudden emptiness. Had it moved right it might have given Kane a chance but it moved the other way, carefully picking its steps around chairs and tables.

Hazy with gin and Kane's punching, the acolyte struggled to separate his gun and hand from the cheesecloth, pulling the stuff over his head. I ground my teeth, grabbing a bottle and shouting Kane to go in. . . .

Then the door opened and in walked a stranger. He was slim and tall and wore an overcoat and wide-brimmed hat and all the brown miming forms melted suddenly away.

Sensing someone behind him the acolyte swung the gun off Kane who grasped the respite and cleared the fifteen feet between in two bounds, reaching for the gun arm. Something cracked.

The acolyte squealed like a little pig as he came over Kane's shoulders because the crack was made by his arm when it broke, the gun falling to the floor where it lay a black and whoreson thing, more consciously and selflessly evil than all the weak evil and dirty naughtiness of the past night. The bishop moved again, and again the blonde hit him with her bottle.

The stranger had drawn back into shadow. The customers were staring in horror, few of them ever having seen the nightlights being systematically beaten out of a human being. Kane's gray passenger was no longer there.

And I knew Kane's long-nursed sleeping fear-spite could kill this acolyte. Not so much for the gangster's well-being did I want to stop Kane; a killing would have us all in court and would automatically send me home as a deportee.

Suddenly I realized I was thinking and seeing clearly again, Larry's bom-bom back inside the piano where it belonged. Then the stranger stepped forward and touched Kane's shoulder, saying something to him, and he stopped his ritual hammering.

This was the end, I knew. I turned to the till, rang up a no sale and took out roughly one third of the night's earnings. When I came from behind the bar I heard Disgracie asking me for a drink. Grabbing my coat and hat I told her to help herself and hurried after the stranger down the stairs.

I lost him. I lost him in the gloom of the garage. I kept my sight on the doors' oblong in case he passed through but saw only the dawn.

With unbelief I watched it press tenderly its mass of light into the mold that was the serrated sky line of the city. I had almost started to believe that night was a constant thing; all time night without contrast—nightlight, starlight, moonlight, or blundering gray lightlessness, but never sun, daylight a switch on a wall.

I watched the customers hurry out into the dawn, and hearing Larry still playing; and hearing with surprise an early Ninth Avenue El going clackety downtown. I had forgotten that this city had people who lived and worked by day as well.

Then I went back to the joint for Abelard. Kane said he was lighting out for Chicago on the first wildcat he could find. I asked him what the stranger had said. He frowned, unable to remember. No one could explain how the man had got in.

We called Larry and he looked up, not knowing the night was over. Surprised, he asked what about the two drunks as he watched Kane lock the door. They can shout or shoot their way out, Kane said.

Abelard came down the tricky stairs quite well. I gave him a drink in the garage. With a flourish Kane counted me out twenty-five dollars and the women sighed at his generosity. I knew he had told them I was a bum he befriended. He was half right. He asked me what I was going to do.

I said I wasn't sure. I was quite sure but saw no point in telling him.

Kane, I said, the difference between me and you is that I know I'm sick and I know how I can heal myself.

His laughter followed me as I led Abelard into the street. I called up Helen to ask her where to park the horse. Listening to her telephone ringing many times I had a few anxious moments until I heard her sleepy voice.

She asked me where Nell was. I said there had been a rough night and suggested that Abelard would never make Chicago and back in an evening. Her laughter did not sound so very sad. She asked me what I was going to do. The conversation went like this:

Why do you have to hitchhike?

Because transport is costly and I see more of the country on foot.

I'm sort of fed up myself?

I can understand that.

I have a car?

Yes?

And we have a hunting box in Canada?

But I don't want to go to Canada—I've been there already.

I heard the laughter of a sleepy frail in morning rut; another spoiled and surly Arachne. Softly I depressed the receiver hook, shocked in a way and sad and unable to understand how she could vomit and then return to it so quickly. There was so much about women I would never know and it hurt me to realize the famous female fastidiousness was little better than a pose. In the gallery of my mind I gave Medusa pride of place and put Helda on the left side and Helen on the right and closed the door.

Spring was busy in the Park as I walked back, my Pegasus safely returned, cold sober. Seeing a clean dug patch of soil I kneeled down on the grass verge and pushed my hands into it.

A cop came up behind me, asking me what I was doing. I told him, showing him the soil and holding it under his nose. He looked at me and nodded. He was a Galway man.

We sat down on a bench and talked about spring in Ireland, how it came on everything in a holocaust of life, how the skies mixed myriad colors on the palette of the mountains.

I sang a good song to this exile and there were tears in his gray eyes when I left him. He was still in the land that I had left forever. I knew now that I had squeezed through a narrow door without a Judas hole to my majority.

# *Not Isaac*

STEPHEN MUIR'S FATHER and the three men on the farm always considered that the boy was soft, especially about killing things. They often joked him, hoping to stiffen him, but only enraging him because he could not explain what he felt about taking an animal's life.

When he crossed sixteen the matter came to a head. And that autumn, when a large pig was being slaughtered for the domestic bacon supply, his softness was clearly demonstrated to all, save his gentle mother.

The three men—Bill Brady, John Conlan and Tommie Maguire—had driven the hog into an enclosed yard where it innocently nosed about, having had nothing but rough care and food from human beings till then. Two of the men had heavy sticks and Brady, a sort of untitled foreman, was armed with a seven-pound sledgehammer. He walked quietly up to the animal, measured it, set himself, and swung the hammer, intending to hit the beast squarely between the eyes and stun it till the throat could be slit.

But the pig moved its head slightly and took the blow on an ear. It fell, struggled, Brady roaring at the others to help him hold it down, Stephen knowing they were half scared of it. The beast got up, throwing the three men off, and staggered round in crazy circles, now knowing enough to mistrust completely Brady and his hammer. Falling and rising and shaking its head as if to dislodge the pain, it squealed in terror each time any of them approached it. Brady was annoyed and the others started to laugh hysterically.

Brady chased after it, the hammer ready for a more damaging blow. They united to drive it into a corner, but the animal seemed to have realized that corners were fatal things and, in spite of the urgent shouts and blows, it persisted in staggering wantonly about the middle of the yard.

Brady lost his temper completely and tried to deliver several random blows as the pig dodged about. One swipe struck the nose and another gashed the sound ear.

Stephen had been watching all this from an upstairs window. Normally, he never interfered with the men and the fact that he was his father's son gave him no authority over them. He felt Brady's hammer blows on his own head and desperately tried to think of a way to help the animal into an easier, quicker death.

Both parents were out and old Tilly Magee, the cook-cum-housekeeper, was deaf as an oak post. Then he remembered that his father had a small old-fashioned revolver in a cupboard. He had often played with the weapon and knew how to use it even if he had never fired a shot.

He found the gun and one ancient shell and ran out with it to the yard. The maimed and bloody pig was snorting in fear and blindly seeking impossible escape, the three men now beside themselves with frustrated, tense rage, their three simple minds locked to the animal as if it must die so that they might continue to exist.

They paid no heed to the boy at first and he had to shout and hold Brady's coat before the man desisted in the crazy chase. He was so full of rage of a different kind that the tears came to his eyes.

The men stopped, self-consciously, their three pairs of eyes staring and bloodshot and, like the pig, breathing stertorously through open, frothy mouths, their lips mauve with anger and exertion. Brady swore coarsely at the animal as if it were at fault for not going quietly to death.

Stephen slipped the shell into the correct chamber in the gun, handing it to Brady and telling him to hold the barrel close to the pig's head. Then he went away quickly and very soon heard the shot. From his window he saw them hurrying from the boiler house with pails of steaming water and knew that the selfless gun had done its duty.

Afterwards, the men probably felt embarrassed about the affair and to cover up they joked the boy more heavily as if their ferine brutality was all of manhood and Stephen's pale face and tears were weak and womanish. Conor Muir was ashamed of his son's apparent lack of pluck, taking it almost as a personal slight on blood and country breeding, as if the boy had stolen something or in some way had brought ill repute upon the house. And he bawled Stephen out for interfering with the old gun, saying it might have blown off Brady's hand.

Stephen said nothing about the pig. His father would have been angry, not in sympathy with the animal, but because the manhandling might have damaged the bacon.

Brady was Stephen's most articulate tormentor; he had

an acrid wit and some self-importance. Conlan was his half brother and Maguire was his cousin. As their fathers before them, they had worked on the farm since boyhood. The three of them were very alike. They had thick, strong bodies, heavy, red necks, long noses with hairy slits for nostrils, and high, narrow heads. Essentially they were brutal. Their lives had asked them for little learning or finesse. To them, as to Conor Muir, a cow was a thing on four legs with an udder for milk between the two hind ones and worth so many pounds.

Finally, to silence and satisfy everyone, Stephen volunteered to kill and dress the Christmas wether, which was always divided fairly between the Muirs and the men for the holiday. The event was to take place on the first wet afternoon of Christmas week as they had been busy with autumn cultivations made late by a stormy November.

For days the weather remained bright and dry and Stephen remembered looking for each sunrise and wishing the day would continue fine. He knew the gentle beast he was to slay. He could remember it as a curly, playful lamb. It was running with half a dozen others in a small field behind the barn. They all had the white face and high nose of the Cheviot and were pathetically harmless and inoffensive. Always they bunched together in the far corner of the field when anyone came to the gate; standing and gazing curiously and nodding their heads, not exactly in fear, but in generic nervousness. When one moved they all moved, seeming to abhor solitariness or isolation.

On the Thursday, four days before Christmas, rain fell all day and at lunchtime Conor Muir said the sheep would be killed. His wife said nothing, looking down at her plate and covertly glancing at her son with a gleam of sympathy in her gray eyes.

After the meal Stephen saw Brady sloping down the fields with the dog, a sack over his shoulders to break the rain and puttees of sacking wrapped around his legs. He seemed to move with overt cockiness as if in anticipation of a diversion.

Stephen went to the old larder with its high racks of wicked hooks from ceiling to floor, reminding him of tales about medieval torture chambers. Even as a child he had always hated the place with its hooks and smells as if the ghosts of the animals it had seen slaughtered had haunted it.

Conlan and Maguire were waiting for the wether to come up, smoking their rank pipes and spreading odors of wet, cow-smelling clothes. As Stephen took off his jacket Conlan asked him how he felt, winking at his cousin. Stephen did not answer and took up the little sticking knife and commenced to sharpen it on the steel.

*Whet-whet! Whet-whet!* the steel said to the knife's unseen edge almost like a bird call. There was a low, strong table like a butcher's block, slightly cupped and black in the cracks with old blood, and the whole larder smelled slightly of rancid grease and carbolic.

They heard the dog bark and the chopping patter of the wether's nervous hoofs. The collie rushed past the beast, turning it back and holding it for Brady to drive into the small walled yard outside the larder door. Conlan and Maguire went out while Stephen waited, his mind now becoming dull and registering every move in slow motion.

There was a slight scuffle over the rain sounds on the roof as the sheep was caught and someone swore at the excited dog, telling it to go and lie down. Then the three men dragged in the victim, one at each shoulder and one at its rump, their big red hands buried deeply in the gray-white fleece. The wether did not bleat or struggle and only slid along the tiled floor on four stiff legs.

Stephen held the knife behind his back, ashamed to let the little animal see it, Abraham and thickets and ancient sacrifices running through his mind. As if the knife itself had bid him he felt his hand tighten on the haft.

The sheep panted with short silent pants, the slitted nostrils moving as the gills of a fish. And its head, its lovely antique head, was wise and beautiful with a terrible and uncomplaining wisdom aware of a long past through which its race had furnished food for knives, bellies, and altars and had heard the sonorous names of long-forgotten gods chanted in gloomy cave, tumulus, and lavish temple.

And its eyes were there, not seeing him nor knife more than another thing. That was the terrible part of it—the virgin, fearless, guiltless innocence. But still he held the knife, the blade against his wrist, for the eyes were gray with kindness, sleepy, and barred with a long jeweled stone of beauty snared in honest opal fire.

"Up on the bench with her!" Brady was saying.

They lifted it with unnecessary roughness onto the block. It lay awkwardly on its side, the four very neat legs stuck out, the neck and head thrown back as if in fatalistic readiness. It struggled a little and they held it down. It did not struggle against fear or hurt or death, but because it was uncomfortable.

Stephen's hand slowly bared the dull fang of knife and he looked down on it. Harlot it was to any man's hand; a cruel, strong thing not made for kindness and healing. . . .

"Come on, me boy!" Maguire urged. "What are ye waitin' for?"

The others laughed. Stephen looked up at them, balancing the knife in his hand, and he could only see three beings holding a fourth down.

Reaching forward his left hand he grasped the beast's satin throat, feeling for the windpipe, then edging his fingers back to the ear, his right hand hardening on the knife haft. Poising the blade just behind the jaw-root, he pressed firmly down without resistance.

The barred eye never changed nor challenged, showing neither fear nor blame. Nor did the body struggle against the mortal wounding. With rigid forearm he pressed the knife home, turning it and outcutting invisibly.

And still the beauty of the eye remained unchanged. Slowly the breathing weakened and blood snored in the lungs, the bright breath-blood dripping slowly from the twitching nostrils with astonishing brightness while the limbs impulsively protested a very little as a worm might curl when a spade touches it.

Stephen withdrew the knife, looking at it curiously, its moist, senseless blade having partaken of a mystery greater than any man might bear, and he was thinking whimsically it was a poor repayment for that first innocent witness so long ago when the barred eyes had gazed on beauty on a mother's knee, their body heat keeping the stable warm. . . .

"Come on! Off with her skin!" Brady was goading, still looking slyly at the others. They had agreed between themselves not to help him, but he knew exactly what to do.

And for him now, the killing over, the beast was no more than an unfashioned stone or lump of unshaped clay.

But his hand was still hard on the knife and sheep smell oozed over his face as he wiped the sweat off with the back of his left hand. The knife locked rigid his forearm and he saw three similar throats, red-necked and slightly hairy with their protruding Adam's apples, arrogant and ignorant, in minds subhuman and human only in form. And he saw three pairs of guileful eyes half-smiling at his lividness and still the ready knife held fast his hand, still poised, greedy, insatiable, ireless. . . .

He turned to the sheep as it moved comfortably and sighed contentedly, the eye still barred in beauty's harmless death. Without direction from Brady, he flayed the carcass and they helped him hang it, then watched him paunch it. Gently the soft gray guts slipped out of the gaping belly-slit, pathetic in the indecent exposure, and still pulsing in their peristaltic action. For their benefit he even decorated the flanks with little cuts that made an ash-leaf pattern on the warm elastic flesh.

When he finished they were full of praise. Suddenly he turned on them, holding the knife blade between his right finger and thumb. Then slowly he raised his arm and flung it with all his strength at the door, the point going deeply, gladly, into the wood and shivering as with life.

Then he took his jacket and walked out quietly into the soft clean evening on which the rain had ceased to fall and a thrush was singing gaily in the sycamore tree over the larder roof in faithful anticipation of the spring.

# The Turning Page

It was in the early spring of my fifteenth year when my brother sent me a clutch of thirteen prize Indian Runner duck eggs snugly packed in soft hay. My parents asked me what I intended to do with them and smiled when I said I would put them under a hen. They thought I was too scatterbrained to take care of them.

At the time none of our hens was broody so I toured the neighbors until I managed to borrow a large white hen that looked to be a good, fierce mother. I took her home under my arm, prepared a nest, and named her Daisy.

She seemed quite pleased when introduced to her potential family, walking unbidden unto the eggs and arranging them around her and covering every one. Once a day I visited her with food and water. Most times she did not want to leave the eggs and I had to lift her off, loudly protesting.

One evening my father came in and told me the rats were tearing at Daisy's coop. I hurried out to find he was teasing me. Daisy was sitting in the darkness and when I pushed my hand under her she pecked my wrist reprovingly. By this time she knew me well; if a stranger disturbed her she would fly at him.

The slow, moist feather-heat of her body was strangely moving to me and her patience and my touch on the smooth, warm eggs. Almost I could sense the quickening movements of the curled embryos within. Muttering, she settled herself over my hand and I could have wept for her faithful flame of life flickering through the nights and days of her long, one-moon vigil.

My life and Daisy's: the twin flames of our lives flickering round the dusty doorsteps of night and day. Loving that old hen, for the first time in my life I felt with fear and pity the great gulf in time between us; and for the first time consciously loving anything for itself, neither seeking nor needing a return.

But the sudden awareness of our difference struck me like a blow. Heretofore, I had moved among men and animals without question, with bare respect or friendliness or fear. But now for the first time I saw them all objectively in their awful completeness. Shuddering at the dream, I held my hand under Daisy for a long time till it too became moist and warm like the eggs, afraid to withdraw it and break the slow life-contact.

The great evening was around me, strangely calm and mild after a bitter day of storm when gales and squalls had lashed the patient earth with proud vehemence, arrogantly bowing every sinewy branch, scattering the rook flocks, and washing widely the squadrons of gulls.

Formless thoughts flitted across the threshold of my consciousness, linking me to the night and the past day; the dark breast of the night upon the eggs of the coming day.

At that age such thoughts frightened me. I was becoming conscious of myself—a small, crouched entity under the triumphant vault of night; my self, crouched on the earth with all things known and unknown around me and under and above me.

So I sat on my haunches, my hand under the hen, the great sky over me racked with cold winds and stippled with stars. The lights were gray-blue and utterly cold, the silent tree forms in supplication against them. The ghost of the sunset flitted across the faces of a few swift clouds, turning them livid: two bold storm thrushes boasted to each other across the darkening fields. Tomorrow I knew there would be more spring dancing and more wind and the trees would press into the dawnlight, refreshed by the night's lull.

The dull fire of the hen's breast still around my right hand, I thought about the red-haired girl with whom I happened to be in love. Many emotions concerning this central spring theme slipped through me; joyful resentment, perhaps, bidding me to move, to take up again the hallowed crucible of my years and continue with my begging bowl to paradise.

Then all emotion would form one—a dumb pain at times outside of me, encrusted with doubts, failures and some longing. Even then I asked myself for the answer to my love, but then as now all that I may see is the face of a beloved staring at me through frustration and preconception.

This love—it is very strange, considering all that supposedly wise men have written concerning it: their books tell me little—only what they thought they thought about

it, not what it is. I can better love with Adam and his Eve
than ruin love with any scholar's sorcery.

The afternoon before that March evening my girl had
permitted me in play to place a hand on her young breasts.
She stood solemn and silent for a moment, hearing my
touch. I had sobbed in my throat for the breast's tender
heat and its still form that my hand could see better than
eyesight, soft as breast feathers. My longing held no shame
nor active lust, no more than young animals who perform
in play the love-act of their kind before their glands are
ripe to consummate a mating.

March changed to April and spring warmth crept over the
fields and woods. Early corn crakes questioned the nights
with their rhythmic, rasping calls. The great flocks of
starlings had dissolved into pairs and already the trebles
of the rook fledglings could be heard from the treetops;
white-vested martins and glossy swallows returned to
occupy again the scene so long familiar to their ancestors;
bats came out from their crowded winter dens to weave their
old, crazy webs of dusk through the blue evenings, and
day- and nightlong the arrowed swifts tore through the
high air as if all flight were joy and all joy flight.

My stream was half full, black and glossy as oil, its
sounds sheathed and sibilant; dry summer would have to
wait for its pebble melody. But all the land was full of
laughter and movement.

The sensitive April skies were reflected on the grass
pools formed a few inches deep by seasonal showers, the
rain water clear, soft, and sweet tasting with the tang of
earth, ice-cold at dawn and lukewarm at noon. Men plowed

and sowed their fields, patchworking the landscape with browns and tender greens.

Each day my fingers felt buds on the low-hung branches, telling their growth to myself, tearing them open to find the close-packed, crinkled leaves within. One miraculous week changed the plum-colored aura of the beechwoods into a mist of palest green, and down through the scrubland, above the lakes, the shepherd crooks of bracken were uncurling. Had I the power I would have stayed the spring at this keen point, prohibiting the flush of June to kill the high expectancy.

And still my hen sat on, so quietly and patiently that sometimes I feared the eggs were unfruitful. My father teased me, saying I would spoil the clutch with too much handling. Everyone at home was amused at my impatience, but everyone was pleased to see my interest in something constructive. I wandered less and as the hatching time grew near I seldom left the precincts of my home for very long. The workmen on the farm were well aware of my absorption. They were always fooling me about it. In their crude eagerness to play a joke they might be tempted to abduct Daisy. I had seen them play rougher pranks than that, entailing grievous harm and death to small birds and animals.

My girl knew all about the eggs and shared some of my feelings; that she could not share them all hurt me. Being a farmer's daughter she was well accustomed to animal gestations. My consuming interest in the clutch amused and puzzled her, and talk as I would I could not offer any really adequate explanation.

On the face of it, I suppose, there was little of note in a

common crossbred hen sitting on a few eggs. I had no words to take the girl beyond the bare physical thing into the moonlit fields of life-love and heart-intimacy.

I sought the lass, she did not seek me, and yet I knew she would watch and wait for my coming, defending me in absence and grieving when I was in trouble; companions had linked our names and parents smiled benignly on our friendship. For myself, I knew not which I loved: April, the eggs, the girl; perhaps I loved the patient Daisy best of all because she served a cause beyond conception without emotion and hope of reward, according to her kind. I could understand Daisy; I could not understand myself or the girl.

Then one morning I ran out to the coop, full of expectancy. If my calculations were correct the hen should be sitting on ducklings. She was very uneasy and talked to herself, resenting strongly my curious hand. Carefully I lifted out an egg.

The shell was intact, but curiously unbalanced, and there was movement within. On my ear I could hear a faint tapping . . . tap-tap, tap-tap, tap-tap; once a safe house, the hard shell was now a prison.

My stomach turned over with emotion. I held the egg in my two hands, the shell now stained and dull: I held life in my two hands: I held spring, beauty, love and existence. Suddenly, I tasted the salt of my tears running over my lips.

Returning the egg, my fingers touched a moist, tiny form under the hen's feathers. Scared to disturb her any further I raced back home with the news and refused to go to school that day.

But it was late afternoon before all the eggs were hatched —the whole thirteen of them. I lifted Daisy off and took away the shell fragments. The tiny golden-brown ducklings were clustered in a corner, wild as mallards, their shrill pipings nearly driving Daisy crazy. Although her patience was rewarded, her life would now be one long worry.

Less than an hour after dawn next morning I was back at the coop and the ducklings were nipping round their foster mother, clean and dry. She talked to them and when I lifted her out she refused food for herself and clucked the feeding call to her brood. The ducklings followed her and she started raking with powerful feet and I showered curses on her, my hair on end, for she flung the delicate little birds all over the place. They knew nothing about scratching for a livelihood and they paid little heed, no matter how invitingly Daisy clucked. They spoke another language.

Suddenly a swallow tippled over the fowl run and Daisy cooed warningly. The effect was magical. The rooster ran about cooing his warning and the ducklings froze against the earth, their heads cocked to one side, looking upward.

The year swung on, turning on jeweled hinges from April into May: May with her hawthorn and cherry blossom and thick mysterious nights of moon-brewed perfumes. April had lured blossom to the blackthorn, but May had far more alchemy and everywhere she touched a flower arose.

Each evening I shut up my ducks and on fine ones I would sit on the wall overlooking the stream and sloping fields, hearing the many-footed dusk approach and stop—

just beyond sight; halting perhaps at the stream and asking what sort of being I was, whether hostile or friendly. O, dusk, I was never hostile!

My red-haired girl wanted to see a duckling and she was too shy to come and see for herself, so I borrowed one from Daisy, put it under my shirt against my skin and set out one evening through the dusk.

My love for the girl had changed and was changing; how it changed I was not aware and I was only dimly aware that it had changed at all. Perhaps my thoughts about her were less poignant, although just as constant; perhaps I had used her as a focus, a center point, round which to revolve my spring, she remaining still when all else moved; perhaps I had partly replaced her with Daisy and the ducklings, moving her slowly outward to the rim of my horizon and therefore sensing change in change of view.

In the beginning of my affection, with the thin, unfurnished threat of spring, each thought for her had hurt with adamant, unvoiced bitterness and my love for her was of the same texture as the hurt. Strangely, I now know my love was a hostile thing—to itself and to us: that much I have evolved notwithstanding the fact that many motion pictures and books make money by attempting to perpetuate an ideal of love that is at most times nothing but the destructive vapor arising from an uneducated and undiscerning conception of adolescent passion and animal affection; our incompleteness misnaming love.

That year my mother read me Walt Whitman's *"Out of the cradle endlessly rocking."* The poem disturbed me and maybe it was one of the causes of my changing love.

In the beginning my love had walked between me and

everything, blinding me with the fulgor of a bigoted vision while always marking my incompleteness and lack of strength. Now, I was attaining a freedom within a freedom and my love was *in* everything: the movement of her limbs and the movement of branches, her smile and a ray of sunlight on a cloud, her voice and the wind's cool laughter in the grasses, her form and the form of any female thing that held the power of procreation and increase. Save for the occult movement of dark, untested passion in my blood, I could abide within myself with less loneliness.

My girl resented my odd moments of complete detachment, although in such moments I was more in tune with everything, and all feeling was more harmonious. I did not know then that females, even adolescent girls, could resent the essential mind's maleness in a man or in a boy. I do not think that women have ever learned to curb the deep Eve-greed in their being.

I had no wish to dominate the run of my girl's mind or to coerce her powers of ideation. I wanted only to share my richer sight and feeling to increase kinship and her own store of ageless wealth. She did not know enough as yet to use her own charms to call me to passion's heel and I in turn did not know enough to woo even for the favor of an early kiss, and love to me meant all of love and passion, nothing barred, ignorant that chaste love-play was half the argument.

And still the stubborn lacery of her conventional mind impeded and delayed me. It dealt with traditional custom and form as her parents dealt, as all our neighbors dealt. The individual who strove even blindly to attain his own stature was an alien being and worthy of suspicion. Consequently, I was named wild, reckless, unstable—even untrustworthy; the last named aroused my resentment. Why, I had never betrayed the nest of a bird and seldom the faith of a friend!

With the duckling in my shirt I ran through the dusk that May evening, leaping on before myself in my haste. That afternoon I had played football and my sinews were loose and free, my wind steady.

The little bird's feet and bill were pinpoints of coldness against my skin; the softness of its down, its tender bone structure, its tiny, hesitant strength like a whisper in an antique tongue linking me to night, to love and to the blessed touch of earth.

I flew down a sloping field through resounding curves of bum-beetles, carefully because of my burden; on under a canopied chestnut whose full flower clusters gleamed waxen against the darkness of massed leaves, along a primrosed ditch where countless blooms were phosphorescent in the green shadow pierced through and through with the lutings of blackbirds: paradise at evenset and not one forbidden tree in sight.

Crossing the stream the duckling moved against me at the sound of water. On I went into a day meadow where the protected grass was knee-high and intimate with night. A mallard rose from under my feet and the dusk soaked up her wingbeats and startled quacking. The duckling sensed its wild kind and moved again, cheeping an answer.

In the meadow the heavy dew seeped through my shoes, making my feet uncomfortable. I took off shoes and stockings, hiding them in the grass and sure of refinding them for I could see my tracks as clearly as footprints in virgin snow.

I ran on, thinking about the wild duck and the night, the free wild wings of the bird and the immensity of night; freedom and night, the duckling against my flesh, the life-warmth of the May earth on the soles of my feet; the stars silent and distant; fragrance of wild mint, sweet grasses and honeysuckle, manna for soft-winged moths that lightly touched my face.

Stopping to listen I heard the wild duck returning, her wingbeats as the plaint of the stream, and I was glad for, when frightened, mallards sometimes desert their nests and let the clustered eggs grow cold and die. After that there was silence, the stream giving mute voice to it, the fields folded in darkness, mice moving through the grass, the rustle of darkness.

A little scared, I hurried on, glad to think about my girl and my half-known desire that was warm and big like the night—a warm, reaching, kindly thing that was compassionate and moral compared to my amoral kinship with the night whose silence was of agelessness and who was the companion of the gods and only friend of man so he could sleep; the silence of cosmic experience beyond all good and evil, all action, all desire, all love: complete and majestic amorality. . . .

I would go softly, each footstep laid softly on the earth; I would go softly near my girl's home and whistle like a curlew and she would come softly. . . .

My whistle, birdlike and natural as it was, disturbed a thousand spirits of the night. Nothing moved, but it seemed everything became aware of my presence, tree

telling tree about me and stars nodding wise bright
heads. . . .

Suddenly my girl came and stood before me, a dark
shape, featureless and unidentified: a form and female in
the night, ageless and unrelenting in its untouched, ex-
pectant womanhood and fit and very necessary for love and
love beyond all check or doubt or blame.

Overcome with strange shyness, awkwardly I produced
the duckling as if some highborn lady of the land had
come from afar to see the little bird. Her hands reached
out, cupping the duckling and my hands. Tenderly she
took it, murmuring how soft it was, how warm, and pressing it against her lips, and the unknown ancestral man in
me well knew that the duckling mattered little to her and
the boy in me resented this.

Then she held it up to the zenith so that she might see
it better. I stood watching her, her two hands held aloft,
a female figure minus name and personality graven on a
dark plate: moving, I caught her profile against a star
cluster. With inward pain bewitched I knelt on one knee
so I could etch forever on my mind the profile—the small
mounds that were her breasts, the lovely unbroken line
running from forehead to chin to breast. . . .

"It's very soft and warm," her voice said again, startling
me, because I had to reassociate her human tones with the
silent, thunderous voice of her form speaking to me in
dark, eternal lines. What sense the voice made meant
nothing to me. I seemed empowered to hear double mean-
ings in a simple phrase; whether the male blood in me
coined the other half I do not know: nor do I know what
answer-question, question-answer flowed between us across

the little space of night that lay between us. A man and woman versed in art of body-love may well anticipate what will be said and done when passion blows his trumpet on the hills.

I did not know what to say and took back the bird, replacing it carefully within my shirt, confused by the abrupt ending of my vision. Then she laughed at me, reaching forward, her cold, quick hand following the duckling. Either her crimson laughter or the touch of her fingers on my chest set me on fire, the sudden, violent return of bodily sensation making me shudder.

In self-defense I caught her arm, but she eluded me and started running. Still hazed by my broken dream I followed, slowly at first then swiftly in the track of her dark movements, almost hypnotically following the lure of her low, exciting laughter as a dog follows scent. My feet were strangely heavy, my mind refusing to take the challenge in the chase, although my body knew its quarry and wished to capture it.

She raced into a quiet little field and at last I caught her round the waist and we fell together on the green earth. In the faint light her ashen face smiling up into mine, her quick breathing touching my right cheek as I looked down into her eyes. They were not smiling. I do not believe I have ever seen the eyes of a woman smile, the eyes themselves; they may be too close to waiting, guile, pain and terror ever to indulge in open laughter.

I was frightened now and cumbersome and awkward, not knowing what to do, for our bodies so close together made us both solemn and the steady purposeful pressure of the girl's body against mine made everything save ultimate contact unworthy. I have often heard a Don Juan rant of his successes with women, but if truth be told, he was never any more than a willing lackey, nose-led by lust and master only by virtue of the physical posture. . . .

We stared into each other's eyes, for me all feeling gathered into one small moment of intensity.

"Mind the little duck!" she whispered.

I started, two ice-cold thoughts sliding together in my brain. My fingers groped for the duckling. They touched it and stiffened, knowing before I did that it was dead.

But her words also implied full consent and she was suddenly quietly relaxed while I was taut with passion and pity for the dead bird. With duck in one hand and a willing girl in the other my mind was split in its intent and passion, pity, and remorse, like three dark birds, sat on the tree above my wooing and never, never flew away.

Relentlessly my desire surged on, I now watching it with dumb regret and some shame, the dead bird still in one hand. Then no longer thinking, I obeyed desire and placed the duckling on the grass beside us, its warm body rapidly cooling, a tiny symbol naming passion when passion was spent.

I have seen the roots of a tender sapling cracking a boulder and I have watched the waves of the sea gouting up a narrow neck of rock, again and again, in gurge and spate. I have listened to the still and mighty balance of trees, their roots spread over the anchoring earth ever unsleeping, ever awake to maintain the perpendicular of the whole. I have witnessed great storms of passion in men **and in** women of all colors and in myself, drunk or sober.

I have seen death come to living things and I have heard death step close to my own soul. . . .

But I am not trying to describe what I felt that night for to do so would be foolish. I sang the song, desire ringing through my body, guideless and unguided, and I died the little death that made possession great and terrible in love's brief ownership that was honey on my tongue and gall to my bowels.

And all the time the woman, my girl—all woman, was miraculously still and took my love till it was ended with an inwardness that had no meaning at all on a man's earth and only touched life because life itself ordained the contact. Then quietly she arose, unchanged, and went away.

I lay alone on the cold earth, passion's vehemence now muddy chaos without purpose. Rolling onto my belly I tried to retch, my face in the wet grass, my hands biting into the soil.

Then after a little while I picked up the cold, moist duckling, stuffed it into my trousers pocket, and crept back through the meadow, tracing old footsteps—how old, how old!

Covered with a dull weariness, I cast behind me the stones of a childish past, tracking old footsteps with a mind so different and raw that it seemed to belong to another person whom I did not know.

I was an unknown man now and not fit to be a man; all boy still, yet master of a man's act; premature experience robbing the boy and maiming the man even as old Adam had been robbed and maimed; outside the gates I was and there had been no need, but how could I know? And how could I know my duckling would die?

I found my shoes and stockings and lay beside them in the grass and slept. The felt rather than heard passing of a snowy owl awoke me. Chilled, I sat up and gazed upon the night—full night now and deep as a leagueless sea around me; in itself a tangible, uncaring form lying close on the breast of the scented meadow.

The Plough's position told me it was about midnight and stars were in the sky I had never seen before. Arising, I dragged myself on, longing now only for sleep and warmth. I could not bother to find the foot plank across the stream and waded through it and in the middle I dropped the duckling. It floated, a pale spot, then swirled around as if alive until the shadows and the waterweeds took it to themselves. . . .

Next morning I relived the entire experience; the mating was strangely indistinct—it seemed its own physician. But I saw starkly again the little form of the duckling swirling into the night. . . .

June came, haytime and time for fledglings to test their wings; meadow-sweet and chaste June roses, gold of gorse, and dark green leaves all ready for the summer sun.

My ducklings had reached the flapper stage. It was their most ungainly age. And Daisy was beginning to lose interest in them. With their increasing strength they wandered further afield. Each evening I shut them up in their little house and each morning I released them. They would feed, drink some water, clean themselves, rest a while, then start down the fields, working their way along for hundreds of yards the daylong and returning to my call in the evenings.

Slowly they became lovely, perfect birds, wonderfully close together as if one mind contained them all. And always their closeness made me remorseful when I thought of the dead one, and so thinking I would think also about the girl.

I had not avoided her, but had seen her only once alone since that evening. We had met on the road one afternoon. She had changed, losing something and gaining something, but what she had gained I did not want. For me, that night I saw her form against the stars with the duckling in her hands, she had died, surely as the bird had died and she had drifted from my life surely as the bird had drifted into the shadows.

She saw my eyes running over her body and blushed for the intimacy it had so freely given me. Although I knew that for the asking she would lie again on the earth for me, I felt no power in the knowledge for somehow I was only able to see the living duckling in her dead woman's hands or the dead duckling in my living hand. . . .

"Michael?" she called as I turned to go.

Her eyes drew mine, I felt her need, and suddenly I think I hated her; not the girl—the leech in her that men call woman. I was armed now and I could look on all women, young and old, knowing what they could give and all that they could take away.

All through the long vacation I stayed with my ducks and learned to know summer as already I loved spring. I never knew a season quite so well before or since. And after that summer my life quickened and they put me into long pants, checking my dreaming and chastising my lethargy at school.

The grain was turning to its dying gold when my ducks discovered the stream. I had always tried to keep them away from it, afraid for their safety, for it led into strange domains where foxes and poachers were numerous and cunning.

But I could no longer deny them their pleasure in the stream. It was their true habitat, their bodies perfectly adapted to it as boats are shaped to fit their element. In it they became graceful, easily moving things delightful to watch in aquatic play; gone was the awkward toddling on feet ill-suited to solid earth. I envied them. I would call no man master could I have found an element so generous to my will.

But the stream's advent disturbed their regular habits and some evenings they did not return. Searching I would find them sleeping in a cluster on the bank or feeding quietly all together in the half-light.

Then one evening when the laborers were stooking the last sheaves in a cornfield of golden, gathering darkness I failed to find my ducks. The workmen laughed at my calling, aping my words and saying quack-quack to one another. I asked them and they said they had not seen the ducks all day. I made them swear on God they had not and when they saw my rage and sorrow they stopped laughing and stared at me.

Diligently I searched over marsh and meadow by the light of a mellow moon, listening for sounds between each breath and footstep.

But O, the quiet beauty of that night of my sorrow. Autumn's great presence blessed the valley, scattering abroad her scents and spices, the perfect alchemist of plenty and fulfillment.

I went home for a meal and searched again and all through the night I sought, quartering each acre of ground along the stream.

Up in the darkness I could hear the mallards' wings hurrying to the gleaning of the stubble fields, the drakes urging the ducks to make haste. The songbirds were silent now and curlews called sadly in the mists over the marshes. Out of weariness and sense of loss I began to win some new peace, as if a page were turned for me by someone who knew more than I. And peace was much more real now than spring's proud, restless satiety.

Calling and listening I followed the stream, stirring carefully each island of flag and reed, until I came to the long lake shore where wavelets chopped up moonlight into a dust of silver on the stones.

Out on the water I heard  a hundred mallards quacking like ducks in any farmyard. Perhaps my ducks had joined them in the safety of the open water. I never saw them again.

# Song of the Barrow

As PERHAPS A beast may hear, over many years the sound was for me a pure percept unconnected with any concept or idea; it was always sad but not ominous. The first time I heard it I was a child on the hazy edge of sense. It came from the coal-house door that had sagged on its hinges and scraped an edge on the concrete floor; then infrequently a breeze might make it by rubbing two branches together, and usually the weathercock above the high ceiling in my bedroom when in the night the wind would veer or back from calm to the wet southwest and coming storm.

It is with me yet, two thirds of my life lived, and now naturally laden with all that memory may endow—an almost archetypal sound, though still uncaught and ephemeral.

I know that springs come and go, the earth opening to the sun like a flower and then dying again; that the seasons pass inevitably, springtime unto harvest; and ultimately I know I will hear my sound for the last time.

May brought life and activity to the peat bogs. In their own right these lake-side bogs were aloof, exciting places, more dead than lifeless rock and yet somehow beyond death; but I never more than half trusted them—they had too many facile moods, even for May, and sometimes they were dour solemn still-silent places where autumn seemed always to lurk in the dense bracken: the mereing lake water deep and peat-stained and ominous, the strands foot-sucking and quaking like a disturbing dream.

When turf time came I prayed through the dull school week for Saturday's weather to be fine, and when the free day came I would rise early and to avoid chores slip away softly across the pasture fields, through the templed beech wood, down the steep hill flank to the first lake; then I could look down on the busy heat-shimmering waste that was the great Rivary Bog, its husbandmen no larger than mice.

One early Saturday I came to Rivary, counting more than a hundred men and boys at work. Some were cutting out, some making mud-turf and shaping the thick-spread glar into loaves with their hands, standing shin-deep in the mud.

This craft of peat-getting was quite familiar to me, had I not mind-known it I would have remembered by blood and bone, each rhythmic gesture an ancient ritual act of kinship to the earth. Half dazed with content I watched the age-old movements—cut, sling, catch; cut, sling, catch —each block of moist blood-dark humus no larger nor smaller than another.

The forenoon almost spent, finally I attached myself to a man I knew, who worked a peat bank with his son's help. The son stood above with wide-fingered open hands, letting the slippery bricks of earth drop easily to rest within them as though he were catching eggs, for when wet the turves were fragile as eggs.

Layer by layer, step by neat step like the unbuilding of a wall the old man worked methodically down the face of the peat seam. It was warm and airless in the hole, and a patch of sweat stuck the shirt to his back. He was a big, powerful, rawboned man with thonged, weather-beaten, age-mottled forearms—an aged man for such a young son. I knew there were seven girls in the family and only this, the youngest, a boy who favored his mother in the face but had his father's high strong Norman nose and big-boned frame.

He was a cocksure youth, which was natural enough with eight adoring women in his home, but he was also pleasant and seriously responsible, conscious of heritage to farm and name. He joked with me as he passed to and fro with his sideless barrow, with one quick tip sliding the turves unto their ends on the heather-stripped spongy sward so they could dry out and drain enough to hold together for windrowing.

And often, guilelessly, he endeavored to impress me that manhood was securely with him and that the four years in his eighteen made him full adult and tied me to boyhood. He walked with arrogance, aware of his broad back and deep chest cage, square wrists and bulging forearms; handling with extravagant ease the heavy barrow, its solid wooden wheel on wooden axle nostalgically ululant, the dolorous sounds taking sides in my mind with a waft of cloud-darkened wind that moved over rush and reed and arced the bees' itinerant flight. I shuddered, anxious with the feeling my mother said was caused by a goose walking over the place my grave would be and making me see always a gray goose with wet, pink-webbed, cold feet.

But a golden swath of sunlight came again, and hands behind head, lying on the warm earth with half-shut eyes I watched him, his fair freckled skin sun-red down to the collarbones and fading to girlish whiteness on his hairless chest; the back of his strong neck a darker red, the rim of light fair hair tonsured by the cap band and made dark with sweat. Like a gage he wore in his cap a sprig of elder, against the early flies that annoyed him when he had both hands on the barrow handles.

Without envy I gloried in his energy, thinking it wonderful to be so strong and capable, so tireless and lightly moving; to be so unerring in the catching of the upspinning peat and so craft-conscious in gesture, hand, timing, and body; to be so free, so close to manhood, his coming and going no longer questioned and his word accepted. Packy was his name—Packy Reilly.

And he became for me a sudden symbol for the May and all of spring's fulfillment: a concrete being but a fit omen for the time; and I was proud of him as I knew the father was proud, and because so obviously did the old man love him, so also did I love him and loved the father for loving so.

By midday the communal fires were kindled and when the water boiled the cooks called. For me the meal was a rural Eucharist. I ate with their eating and filled myself with their satisfaction. They were all hungry and tired, some of them not having tasted food since dawn, for many came to the bog from afar. Before the bread's breaking each one removed his headgear, the older men doing so with embarrassment and rubbing hopeful hands over naked domes, still not convinced after so many years that their hairs had gone for good.

The Reillys shared their food with me. I knew beforehand their butter was sweet and not rancid. The open fires gleamed genially, the flames making fairy whirlpools of hot air that swayed the hazel canopy overhead. Replete, the men lolled back and smoked, talking of other bog days with slow memories that might have been their own or those of past ancestors. I larked with the younger lads for half an hour, jumping bogholes and battling with turf-sods.

In the hills' lee the flat of marsh and bog was hot as August and after the windrowing I walked carefully to the lake's edge to bathe and saw the darkness delve down fifteen feet to a weed-green bottom, a sublacustrine world of eel, salmon, perch, bream, and insensate pike; airless, aloof, and somehow more frightening than the gray rock-rimmed restless depths of the sea-loch. And again, unreasonably, I heard the peat barrow's nocturnal wheel-song, two lugubrious notes it had, like the ass just then braying; a little minor chord, maybe B-flat and E. It moved across the bog; twoscore other barrows sobbed similarly and a hawklike cuckoo made the swallows give their low two-noted warning that was the same tone as the barrow song; all sounds flowing softly down into this little hollow of music.

But I gazed about, satisfying myself that May was still safe and sound in sun, wind, and cloud. And then I first saw the bream. I thought a hand of wind was fingering the oil-calm surface but then I saw the dorsal fins slicing the water. This was the first bream school I had ever seen, this little mad miracle of countless sperming fish troubling the water. I crouched staring, knowing normally they were shy and secretive bottom feeders and now bold and careless in their seething shoal. They bore inward till I could see their forms and distorted shadows in the sunlit shallows: large and small—some of the big ones twenty pounds. I wanted to keep them to myself but I also wanted to catch them and could not catch them all. Turning to the bog I shouted, cupping the call with both hands and throwing it aloft like stone from sling.

"Bream! Bream! A school—a school!"

I might have sworn ransom to the first who reached me. Every man and boy downed work and doubled over, falling swearing laughing in their haste and splashing into the water beside me with staring eyes and open mouths and chests heaving with the race. I got out of the way, for they scared me a little, reminding me of tales I had read somewhere about mobs trampling living bodies underfoot.

Excitement owned them all; uncaring, they plunged after the bream, slashing with sticks, sleans, and forks; falling over each other, inadvertently hitting and hurting each other so several petty scrimmages arose, as if they were also drunk with life and May and obeyed a race law in primitive abandon, the rut-drowsed fish quite lost in the splashing.

Packy Reilly was in the van, the first to catch a big one with his bare hands, kneeling belly-deep in water and holding up the curving life-arc in unconscious Protean mime. Now and again a big flat brown form rose through the air and bounced on the grass, pitched quivering off fork prongs or half stunned with sticks. Soon twoscore and more fish flapped on the grass, slapping against each other, enduring agony, their element but a few tragic feet away.

Slowly the wild enthusiasm died down as belatedly the bream reacted to danger and moved out into deep water. One by one the exhausted humans waded ashore, now slightly self-conscious in proportion to their years. They started stripping and wringing out their clothes.

"Packy! Where's Packy?" a strong imperious voice demanded. "Packy!"

Talk, laughter, and all movement froze save for the slip-slap of the dying bream. All heads turned to old Reilly, then to each other wonderingly as if they'd been asked an awkward question. They looked about, over the grass by their feet, behind each other as though big Packy were a hop-o'-my-thumb and crouching at an instep; but they never lifted an eye to the lake.

"Packy! Where is he?" Reilly roared, his staring eyes wide-shot with fear. He caught a neighbor's arm and bellowed Packy in his ear as if the man were hiding the youth for a poor joke. Then he listened to the stark silence through which tripped faintly off the scrubland the name and came lightsomely, gaily back—Packy! Packy! Packy!— answering itself each time with many voices more faintly, faintly, faint until it also wearied of the search and fell silent; but not for me. The name Packy had leagued with the barrow's two-noted song.

They all wasted seconds to arrive perforce at the same frightening conclusion; not so much wasted as ill spent the time in case there might have been a happier answer. Every eye now moved reluctantly to the mud-stirred lake and I saw again the dull depth-fall to the green bottom that could have as many feet again of liquid mud under the weeds.

With a startling animal howl Reilly ran into the water. He forced his thighs against the increasing pressure with grotesque high prancing: falling flat, disappearing, rising, surging on, his shirt now flimsy and clinging to his frame as the sweat had stuck a patch of it to him in the boghole. As a lash his wailing seared me with new guiltiness, for his cries had the same pitch and cadence as the barrow's dirge and the ass's bray, and Reilly now choired requiem for Packy and also for my May.

Two neighbors ran after him, catching his arms, talking and trying to restrain him. They knew he could not swim.

"Let me out!" he mouthed. "Lemme go, God damn ye, lemme go!"

He struggled, all friends now enemies, spraying the water into a rainbow. . . . "I'll kill ye if ye don't let go of me! Packy. . . ." The two men closed in and he gave up, sobbing and so spent that they had to half lift him back as if he had just been rescued.

Three other men, strong swimmers, had stripped and gone into deep water. Their black heads bobbing like otters at play, they dived together, round white backsides turning up as they disappeared, and then again and again the black heads bobbed, gasping and spewing, taking fresh breaths and going down again. One man waded in exhausted, saying something about being caught in the bottom weeds and all heads nodded wisely with knowing ayes of assent droning like an amen. The man was vomiting noisily, his ridged rippling stomach going flat and hollow with each painful retch.

The other two persisted, coming up, going down—black heads, white bodies, bubbles and writhing water that still seemed harmless under the sun. Then one surfaced and made signs to the shore with his right hand. Voices said: "They've got him!" A boy who knew no better cheered and someone clouted him. He fell head over heels and began to snuffle and another lad sniggered. I wanted to laugh as well, although I knew laughter would now be weeping.

Old Reilly paid no heed and sat whimpering on a stone, muttering now not his son's name but the name of his wife over and over again: Bridie, Bridie, Bridie . . . as though asking her for comfort while attempting to make up a reasonable story, his craggy peat-stained hands fumbling over his shining bald head—doubtfully, as though he had already disremembered what he had been starting to say to his wife and did not know how to set about re-thinking it.

His grief disturbed everyone. They glanced at him shyly —ashamed and scared of him and his sorrow, and wishing he would take it somewhere else. They were fully sympathetic but quite unable to measure or match with approximate agony the agony of his wild suffering. They all knew as I knew that Packy was his only son and last one, the mother no longer fit to bear again. And as dogs will sometimes rend a howling injured companion, the old man's remote despair and the distant grumbling mystery of it angered them and made them impersonally hate him.

I knew none of them could think clearly above the storm of the mourning; they were not hard men but none was subtle; it filled their heads like shells' sea-sound, muting the near and stately tread of death. Nervously the fathers sought for sons with their eyes and gratefully named them in health.

The divers had gone down together, staying down a long time, the witnesses holding their breaths as well and only exhaling when the men broke surface and turned to the shore, one stroking with his left arm and the other stroking with his right, their right and left hands towing something heavy.

All the spectators made cross-signs, glancing furtively at the father in case he noticed their premature fatalism. For the heavy thing between the swimmers offended them all and I sensed they would as soon have left it there in the weeds under water. One older man went quietly to Reilly, bending down privately to whisper the news; but he was not heeded nor heard at all and Reilly's sorrow-surly in-difference to Packy's reappearance seemed to concede victory to death.

The divers had dragged Packy into shallow water, the boy coming in face down, his head hanging between hulched shoulders. They gladly gave him up to the dozen men who met them.

A hundred yards out the bream school still milled about, death-indifferent in life-lust. My mind turned over every-thing again: Packy, May's prototype and now like the

stranded fish; the fish chastely life-lusting to their own increase with pallid sperm sinking grayly unto myriad cold
eggs that would hatch under the sun's breast and make
more fish for other Mays. I glanced nervously at the clump
of men and boys, all of them male and hard-lined like
myself, muscled and set and manned to beget and suddenly
I saw not males but females gentle-breasted and watching
Packy's form with anxious eyes, wise in their sorrow.

I shuddered and looked for relief over the fields, lakes,
hills, and distant mountains anchored in the sea. . . . I
could only peer at Packy from the corner of an eye,
ashamed to stare openly, the youth now a stranger and
something quite secret and personal.

Instead, I watched the two weary divers and their lean
living bodies, their red necks and forearms as Packy's neck
and forearms had been sun-red. One of them held his nose
in forefinger and thumb and cleared his ears, then blew
through each nostril with small tearing sounds. The second man copied and both started to jog up and down to
keep warm. Old Reilly moaned and swayed on his stone.

Packy had been laid face down on a round boulder and
two men were pumping his arms, a third astride his but-
tocks and rising up the ribs with his hands much as hands
were held, thumb to thumb, when shaping the magma of
mud-turf.

The wet pants and shirt cockled wryly on the body, the
taut proud muscles now lax and flabby. . . . I could hardly
understand. I had seen death coming to animals but there
had always been blood; now there was no blood—just pale
loose laxity. And I was disturbed because the abandoned

lying of the form to the earth made me see little difference between earth and form, the blond hair now dank beaver-brown with young green waterweeds in it and a garland gage of weeds wound round his waist.

The sobbing father paid no heed and the men kept working on Packy. The men round the body looked at each other and shrugged, and one by one the observers removed their headgear and the old men still ran tentative hands over their bald domes: this not for the bread's breaking.

No one noticed my departure and that it was unseen seemed ominously condemning. I stepped over the dying still-living fish that smelled faintly of lake mud, their gills hopelessly gnawing the cruel air.

Looking back, I saw the knot of men and boys, resembling flies gathered on a mirror against the lake-caught sun. By the roads, I told myself. I will go home slowly this day by the roads and maybe find a man or woman or young fair girl going my way and we will talk and walk together and listen to each other's livingness.

A wild duck startled me. Absently I stopped to count the blue-washed eggs thinking that if there were ten Packy was dead but if eleven he was alive. There were eight eggs as the bird flew swift and low to the lake, banking across the mourners and glancing over the scrubland like a bullet. I knew she would faithfully orbit her nest until I went away.

Distance knitted now and the bog men seemed to merge into one small motionless figure by the strand. Two martins with very white vests came together overhead: turning as one, then treading the air and coming beak to beak, chuckling to each other at the mallard's foolishness and fear.

This world of nature was once my whole world and demiparadise; no other angel present save the kindly ones that graced me to live peacefully with any beauty eye could discover; no sickness, sorrow, nor affliction, no suffering nor death: all humans no more than young and old and only incidentally male and female by shape and member as animals were male and female.

A bird might fall through age or accident, hawks took their due toll, foxes seized weakling lambs and gulls and gray crows picked the white bones, stoats lusted after rabbits: but these were all natural departures and deaths, if deaths at all; life thriving at the expense of life with reason and unknown purpose much as leaf-fall fed the next budburst: these were the slow eternal things, as the year was and the seasons; one might not waste too much pity on them.

Old people lived stiffly safely on and babies thrived; and although the parish sexton—that round-backed ancient with gray quiet points for eyes, always with red sub-earthly clay under his long nails—although he often marked with lingering bell a neighbor's passing, he also tolled imperatively for worship, joyously for marriages, and contemplatively for the angelus.

I passed an old elderbush and pinched off a leafy crown, smelling the sap-sour scent of the wounded stem. Packy's gage had been elder and I examined the plant, feigning interest in it but only to beg time, to delay what I now had to think while not knowing how to think, since I had no concepts ready to fit my feelings in this new territory of my soul. I was only a boy, and yet no man might guide me here save that which for well or for ill was the becoming man in me.

Crushing the fetid leaves in my hand I faced the change at last in its unresolved totality and acknowledged for the first time that my world was also full of people—humans, humankind—not only inhabited by shadows, fixed institutions, and the elemental movement of wind and star. Tears were running down my cheeks and not all of them for Packy nor for myself nor for my May but for strange self-loneliness.

Down by the lake two dots that were men led a larger dot that was a horse and cart toward the strand, and I knew this was to be Packy's bier and May's bier and bier also for fourteen feckless years of life that counted infant, child, and boy. And I knew the cortege would wend slowly up the valley, Packy lying on the cart's scratched dusty floor, the unsprung ironshod wheels sinking to the naves at times in the ruts cut deeply in the peat and jolting his head and jerking his limbs as if he tossed in sleep; maybe he was still asleep, or reborn, or undying into death as the bream took time to die.

Perhaps the men would think kindly to strew the cart's floor with rush and marsh mint and wild thyme and line the box with asphodel and pearly ropes of hawthorn and set a sprig of elder between the horse's ears to drive away the flies.

And soon now the church bell from its high place would

clang across the parish, lifting all heads to hear, between each slow strike, its own long-dying note—the sound of the barrow's trundle-song and the scrape of the coal-house door of my childhood and the first wild world-cracking shriek of an infant.

# Narcissus Unto Echo

As THE NURSE pulled back the curtains the morning light had the same taut starched texture as her overall, and Stephen Muir knew that snow had fallen before the tall auburn-haired girl turned from the window, saying something about the weather.

"Yes, I know," he said.

"You haven't been out of bed?" she asked sharply.

He shook his head. "No—no need." He smiled. "I sort of heard it."

She looked at him, frowning.

"A speck of thistledown makes a noise, y'know," he muttered. "Almost like the passage of a great ship to a gnat."

She lifted her eyes off the bed chart and glanced at him doubtfully, trying to read into the night nurse's normal entries a reason for his remarks.

"How are you this morning?" she asked, coming round the end of the bed.

"Fine," he whispered, opening his mouth for the thermometer she was shaking.

"Please don't bite it!" she warned sternly, and he shook

his head, slightly irritated and expecting her to divine that he now lay no longer in his usual valley of despair, but floated instead on a wind-braced, open moor of mind. He did not feel the thermometer leaving his mouth, his thoughts returning to their themes that all made pathways back to the Old Mill as if it were a central shrine in a puzzling maze.

He knew that snow and his memories of the Old Mill had only the slight connection that many years before he had helped carry his mother's coffin out of the dark, warm church along the cemetery lane and into the stinging bluster of a January squall that had lashed the escaping flakes across the shrouded graves and flapped the cleric's surplice, almost indecently exposing his long black-clad legs.

And when the priest had said earth to earth he could not find the little morsel of soil the sexton had laid by for him and had picked up instead a pugil of stained snow, letting it fall in one putty lump into the grave's blank openness, and soon the few shivering mourners were all gray ghosts no more in life than any of the livid monuments. . . .

Snow and nostalgic formulae: each year uncovering small forgotten points so that slowly his broken memory learned to heal itself and taste and feel the touch, smell and taste of events that had happened only once so many years before. . . .

The doctor came in and talked with the nurse and they gave him an injection. Whatever it was, it made his body comfortable but left his mind more free, and he was grateful to the drug for stilling his body's lawless chatter and giving his mind oiled, powerful pinions without impediment.

This was snow time again: white snow and its silence that was inborn, clamorous noise born from the chill gray hearts of ominous clouds; each flake a paving stone flung on the earth; and all a world, a universe, removed from summer.

And underneath the snow, perhaps the earth her own dam lived close with death and faithfully prepared herself for yet another spring, culling in simple darkness all her sweet spices and savors for summer's golden manor; maybe the earth was like an old and weary wheel turning and turning in the flowing of a constant sun, hour by slow hour, high day, work day, and holiday.

He knew now there could well be no rhyme nor reason in the blind outreaching of a boy's mind that was checked only by the days and events; by rain, perhaps, and wind, by seasons and all the games from conkers to flying kites in the gales of March. So many things a boy does have to learn; there is no end to early newness and each new thing mated with the old and made new again.

He reasoned critically that to a small spider a cord of gossamer might well be as important as a steel-spun rope is to a builder of bridges; and a loosely spoken word or thoughtless action well might have effect far beyond the careless intention of the actor.

That holiday with his aunt had had three events to do with major adult life: firstly, there was the first evening when he had come upon William bouting the servant girl in the barn; then in the fourth and last week there was Mistress Tully, a widow and neighbor. She had got herself a child by a laboring man and came to her time when working in a harvest field. Stephen had been sleeping in a stook in the afternoon, drowsed like the poppies in the sun fumes. He had awakened suddenly to the new cry of a child and had watched Mistress Tully bear the child and cut the thick red cord and make a cradle out of sheaves and then continue to work to keep the neighbors from her shame, although they all knew months before. He had crawled over and had looked down on the sleeping babe, which made its nipple mouthings even in sleep, and then he had found the afterbirth wrapped in a torn petticoat; and when he had asked his aunt about it all she told him curtly to mind his own business.

And on the fifth afternoon of the holiday he had wandered into her room when she was preparing herself for the weekly trip to town. It was like that in the beginning. He could not keep away, he loved her so.

She was washing her tall white form from a green china bowl, the matching ewer on the floor, the room full of her savor spiced with soap, camphor and apple scent from the loft above, all blended into her sweet personal odor. He did not see her then as a woman, the mate of his sex. He was only twelve. But in the dim bedroom she was an exciting, magical thing shining in her own splendor, and his eyes followed faithfully the loud beauty of her, sculpt in flaming lines that ever after held their fire, giving him a nude prototype for female health and vigor.

Perhaps he loved her then all ways. With honesty to himself he did not know, having no word to say for love nor having the lover's possessive art: agape for beauty, perhaps; not Eros for physical possession.

She did not speak, but turned aside a little and swiftly rubbed her body with the half-concealing towel; not wishing to evidence haste while making all haste. Quickly she pulled on shapeless vest and pants, sitting down on the bed and asking pleasantly and self-consciously if he would like to go to town with her.

He declined because her furtiveness enraged him and he resented she could only speak freely in some clothes, denying him the pleasure her full honest beauty gave him of itself. He could not then think out these things, but nevertheless he knew them.

Before William, the servant man, led the high gig out of the cobbled yard she asked again teasingly if he had changed his mind, as if she were aware of his feelings and tweaked them, now all smart and dressed up and self-assured.

He declined with a headshake and wandered down the old orchard, sitting beside the rock-cut well to count the hours till she returned.

The well's deep eye stared blankly at the sky. It always scared him a little as if the living water were alive with a kind of reptilian consciousness. Again and again in the cool mirror he saw her pale form and superimposed upon it his own features, the water's quiet breathing, her breathing and his own, each breath in unison. Taking a handful of stones he dropped them on the water, shattering the images and watching the ripples blend his own reflection with the other, distorting both, and mocking the encircling rock. . . .

As he remembered it, his aunt had auburn hair of stronger, brighter dye than the day nurse's hair. A tall woman she had been, with eyes that were green and yel-low-flecked, the flecks storming together and making the eyes dark and sulphuric whenever she was upset. On his cheek her mouth was large and moist, her breath sweet. After a kiss he expected to bear the brand of her lips, so red they were.

Sometimes she was sad within herself. Her husband had been hurt in the war in France and was a prisoner. She did not know then nor did Stephen know that he had been wounded in the genitals and that she had a eunuch for a mate. This knowledge came to Stephen later and blended with all the other negative symbols in his mind, begetting incestuous images that ghosted on the endless calms of his frustrations which gentleness or violence failed to dispel.

Then there was the Old Mill. On the first day of the visit he had been sternly forbidden it. His aunt's hardness on this one point puzzled him, and she offered no reasons. William and Bridget, the servant girl, refused to be drawn into any explanation. Perforce he accepted his aunt's au-thority and perforce he questioned it: all summer paradise save for a solitary meaningless prohibition?

Years later he had learned that his great-uncle had given the Old Mill to a family of tinkers because he was playing with their women. These people had built themselves a hovel inside the great roofless walls. His uncle was also a wild man and he had had a tinker lass at the mill, even after marriage.

These scraps of hearsay fused into his memory of his aunt, her dislike for the mill and her loneliness beyond his healing. Set in the lovely ouch of a summer's day the cruel lure of her frustrated beauty branded him and he knew he had always sought to refind her as a mother in other women's love, wishing them all redheaded aunts and close with the ineffable blood intimacy that makes flesh one and comes, perhaps, only after years of marriage.

It was like a fairy story told by a wandering doting crone who laughed and carelessly contradicted herself each hour, saying white bird, black bird, without regard to truth; myth built on baseless myth; faiths life-made and broken, yet never losing life; mirrors echoing perfectly the image, but always the master image out of sight; source origins of power worn frail by check of circumstances and soiled by use, misuse and usury. And yet he knew these worthless and nostalgic dead would never once admit for him self-burial.

Perhaps, even, it were all self-love and he was an oaten Narcissus at one remove, unable to pass freely through time's meniscus and taste all food and drink without restraint. Narcissus knew at least that once the ripples slept he would return again in beauty.

Like a child nibbling round the bun's dull parts till nothing remains but the icing, in a very few days only the Old Mill remained unvisited, his fondness for his aunt no whit soiled by the inevitable disobedience.

Not that he had not joyed in the farm and its complex life: the strong sweet smell of the young red bull with its great male's neck and head, its manly mastering of the drowsy cows and the swift, clean mating stroke and the surge of its great bulk much as a wave bruises a receptive, uncomplaining shore; the farther fields rich in their growth unto harvest, dressing their aloof beauty at the command of any kindly wind; roadside, laneside, and rough stone wall graved with the crisp hieroglyph of moss; military fields of flax where small blue butterflies danced daylong as if the blooms had wearied of their stems and took the air for freedom; the tiny movements of the golden-crested wrens creeping like shuttles weaving into summer's tapestry the large impatience of the spring: love life and love laughter all warped into a thousand dainty patterns and every motif a hymn to the sun. . . . No summer since had known such magic, no evenset or start of dawn so clear and chill, no field more friendly.

He wandered down to the old orchard and sat beside the well, waiting till he heard his aunt set off on the weekly trip to town. Twice she called his name, but not even did Narcissus answer within the well's moist cave. He knew that William and Bridget would be occupied with loving, and when all was quiet he went down to the mill lane, acting a nonchalance in case someone might track his intention.

Once a busy way active with heavy carts, the lane was now grassed over and very silent, close-cropped by nursery rabbits and pitted by scrapings where they dropped their pebbles of dung. The tall hedges and hedgerow trees denied the sun, staining the way a solemn secret green shadow-savored with mint, meadowsweet and moist humus as mossy graveyards often smell in summer rain.

With feigned innocence he stopped to watch the dragonflies course up and down the aisle and prey on the mists of gnats surging like puppets on a thousand strings each time their destroyers spurred through them. Witlessly they danced and danced their mazy measures unmindful of mortality in inane joy without end or beginning and bounded by a day.

The lane widened round a slow curve and he came upon a high wire fence stretched tightly across. He climbed the fence after a full five minutes of hesitation, his chest tight with increasing apprehension, fully expecting anything from dusty ghost of long-dead miller to irate aunt in prancing gig, but nothing moved save a score of tiny rabbits that were so strange to humankind they almost let him handle them as they bounced in and out their burrows like curious gamins giggling round a door.

Ahead like a lost church he saw the mill's gray oblong in the shade of a dense stand of gnarled beeches. Cracking a rotten twig sharply underfoot, an echo came clearly back, startling him a little, and for a while he played softly with the sounds, never before hearing such a clear reflection. Around him crept a faint aroma of wood smoke, melting into all the other odors and making one cloying single scent that ever after associated itself with death and dying.

The swift deep stream still slid obediently through its worn race, toying indifferently with the great wheel's rotted spokes that clung to their mighty shaft, faithful to the time when grain ran free and rich as gold between the slow and runic stones.

But for the water, leaf rustle and the long cooing of an amorous quest, the afternoon was wholly silent. He played by the stream, telling himself to play by the stream, where the outrace joined it, wanting to mark its nearer side his limit and then return, half-satisfied, his aunt's command but half-broken.

He watched his flow-moved features and a cloud of minnow shivering and moving as one fish each time his shadow threatened them. And as the dragonflies charged through the gnats so did a small pike, gray as a curse, rush through the minnow, completely dissolving them. But in a second's time they reassembled, using the stream's flow with the same witless concentration.

It was a very pleasant place, but as if restrained by sickness he could not free his mind and free his body for behind everything he saw and felt he heard the obdurate echo of his aunt's no and saw her full red lips ringed around the word, pinned on his consciousness by an admonishing forefinger as if she were a goddess worthy of fear as well as love.

To keep his faith with her he wanted to turn back, but somehow turning back would break faith with himself and as from a great height he watched his stubborn thoughts reach out and test each tardy footstep braced in readiness for flight and seeing another person slowly walk around the mill's tall gable.

Beyond the wall's strong shadow he plunged into sudden full flaming sunlight and was discovered, felonious and ashamed. Blinking, he tried to find a focus for his sight and found, as once he had found his aunt, the beauty of a young girl who washed herself in a bowl of water on a tree stump in a grassy yard beyond the mill.

She was naked to the hips; breast dropped neatly alongside breast, shoulder and arm line ice white in sunlight; forearm, neck nape, neck pillar. . . .

Fully accepting this appearance as reward, he stumbled forward to greet this being, this guarded princess born of sun and shadow alchemy, his hand outstretched to touch gratefully an arm, or with a jealous index finger to enline lightly the power of the spine groove, molding a form perfect again in his mind's members without denial till each endless gesture gathered up complete familiarity and peace. . . .

He meant no sacrilege. He wanted peace, not knowing that he wanted no more than eye and touch might take and take away to store as rune against the time when manmade deserts denied even the generous giving rain and tears. For in that timeless point he saw all his life, tasting the thwarting of ambition by hard-won thresholds, all paradise regained save for a single law which to obey contaminated all of paradise; a hopeless hopeful waiting in anterooms of dream. . . .

Unseeing, he tripped and fell into a clump of nettles that hid a mound of rubble. Through the sting's spiteful ire on hand, knee and face, he heard a hard voice ask him what he wanted there.

It was the mother of the girl, or the girl's nurse, guardian or jailer—a tall, spare young woman with hot, resentful eyes in a lean, sad face. Large golden earrings dangled against her neck, the sun exactly behind her head. That was all he saw for her eyes burned their suspicion into him, doubling his trespass as if she were his aunt's second embodiment, which indeed she was in that she was also aunt by blood.

"G'wan! Git out'a here!" she barked, more in a warning than in anger, pointing back the lane, her right arm dominant with all of banishment.

He frowned, embarrassed, rising to his feet and trying to say he meant no harm. But the rigid arm did not relax and he wondered at the brusque brutality of her desire for privacy.

Their voices turned the girl to them, the sun-clean pivoting of her body bringing tears to his eyes for she flung a spate of babble at the woman, coming over quite careless of her nudity as a beast is careless; her carelessness offended him even as his aunt's furtiveness offended him.

Her features moved him to pity and horror. They were brute coarse and empty of any emotion but unceasing squint-eyed meanness, the pendulous lower lip maiming her speech, the long upper lip split in a toothy snarl and stiff with black bristles.

"Git out'a here!" the woman snapped again, her eyes shrewdly measuring the narrowing distance between the advancing girl and the boy. "L'ave him alone, Janey!" she snarled, moving to face her daughter.

The girl was slobbering words that seemed curses, her body now shaking with a venom past all reason. Stephen could not move, knowing somehow she hated him and his staring, but unable to withdraw his eyes. To be so starkly conscious of her and yet to look past her seemed greater insult. Dumbly he held out both hands, marveling in spite of all at the easy balanced upsurge of each perfect breast as if the great artificers of form had relented in their spite once they had completed her poor mockery of features.

But the mother was shouting at the girl and shaking her fist, dodging from one side to the other as the girl dodged.

"Git to hell out'a here!" she hissed at him in desperation, grasping her daughter's wrists.

As they struggled he turned away, hearing them panting against each other, their bodies straining grotesquely.

Then the girl broke free and charged him almost as the pike had charged the minnow. He covered his head with his arms to take her clawing blows. The mother tried to come between them, but the girl grabbed his hair with both hands, wrenching him off his feet and kicking at him. Then she snatched a stone and tried to jab him with the pointed end, bending over him, a prehistoric fury, clumsy yet animal clean and swift in movement, her rage no more personal than a bull's rage or a dog's. Puzzled by the violence he curled up on the ground like a hedgehog.

Before the stone could fall with truer stroke the woman locked her thin brown arms around the girl and tried to lift her bodily away while hissing again at Stephen to go.

Savagely the girl writhed, her white body now scored and blotched. She bent forward, throwing out her rump and lifting the woman's feet off the ground.

"God damn ye!" the mother ground out through straining jaws, shifting her grip, her two nut-brown hands biting into the girl's breasts and grasping handfuls of soft flesh for better purchase. Stephen shuddered as the girl bellowed with pain and gave ground, her roaring bouncing off the mill's echoing walls and flying round and round his head like bats in a cave.

As if he had never learned to walk, he crawled away on hands and knees. Then he got up, stumbling, running, hearing their fierce argument and then the sound of blows.

As one hunted by insensate furies he raced along the lane, seeking on either side a hiding place, but the thick hedges with their barbed mesh of brier showed no opening till the tall fence halted him, the wires shrieking in the rusted staples as they took his weight.

Plunging into a field of tall corn that was wounded by
poppies' redness he lay flat, sobbing and covering his head
in hurt and shame, his face against the earth, hardly knowing that he wept or why he wept, the head-heavy grain
leaning curiously above him and watching and whispering
in sedate amaze.

It was not the immediate violence that affected him; it
was the shrouded, old, dammed-up violence of it all that
still clung to him as a cloak; violence that would not cease
with inactivity but would brood on and on. He did not
know how he could face his aunt and wished the holiday
were ended to end deceit, for he knew the ensuing weeks
would be tinctured with duplicity, all love and beauty
bitter.

But while empty of everything but doubt, he was still
stubbornly aware that truth within the frozen lines of
beauty's form needed neither secrecy nor defense; guilt
gave and took offense, not innocence . . . but yet behind
all beauty there was violence asleep; a kindly summer sun
was also stellar holocaust, and the gentlest summer breeze
might nurture hurricanes.

And now he knew his summer's course had run and
autumn had already mortgaged all his days to winter that
never knew a bird had ever sung or foraged for a nestling;
life an inevitable tide leaving him lying like a stone upon
a weary shore. . . .

Some saint had said somewhere that to merit heaven a
man must first make peace with life: but life itself—choice,
chance, or chaotic mingling? His life, even his own, was
but his own idea of life. . . .

He knew the man as man and boy had never tasted

solace for himself in this and knew that he should have been awake to dream as Adam dreamed his rib to Eve, not seeking beauty's lair behind a broken common law. He could not mend the law he broke. . . .

No other course now but cling to resurrection, where in due and mysterious time he might see and know his mother once again, seeing her whole. As a colt fears fire he had feared his handsome violent father and never loved his mother on this earth. She was deformed by illness all his days, falling out of life at last as a wizened crab apple drops from its useless branch, its taste still fierce and acrid even in decay. . . .

He shrugged and smiled to himself, comfortably relaxing; as much good saying no to a new moon had his aunt but known. "But how could she know?" he mused forgivingly. "And how could I know?"

Idly he considered that to have wonder without reverence was to know distrust and fear and so use life as if it were a drug, hating it and craving it. . . . He knew at times he had been sore afraid of death, smelling afar its sweet and sickly stink. How foolish!

"A mist of gnats," he muttered gently. "A stream, a cretin's nurse, a summer day, a nostril plugged with clay and saintly beauty made the quiet sport of worms. . . .

"No . . . not so!" he denied, starting up and wondering at his lightsome ease of movement and hearing from very far away the words return. . . . No . . . not so! Not so!

Lightness and strength increased in him and, surprised at the surpassing gentleness of the transition, he watched the nurse come in, move swiftly over to test his sightless eyes and then reach for his pulse.

"But I am not there," he said to her quizzically, watching the thin red cord that tied him to the form upon the bed grow weak and suddenly snap with a start of exquisite pain.

The nurse did not seem to hear. Dealing so much with death and dying he knew she believed in them and could no longer envisage health.

Lightly he touched a frond of auburn hair in gratitude and turned to the window. Surprised, he passed easily through the barred frame and savored the air's white clean tang. The snow had changed the world's old face, smoothing out all cruel contours and masking with its chaste shroud time's deep-cut lines.

"This is the year's good time," he muttered restfully, pleased with himself. "The harvest's home and the earth's asleep."

Down on the lawns several of the other inmates were playing and marveling like children in the snow. One of them was rolling in it and laughing loudly, grasping armfuls of it, eating it and rubbing it over his face. Stephen came beside him, laying a restraining hand on his shoulder. The but-half-embodied maniac felt the restraining hand and cocked his head like a bird.

"Not that way, brother," Stephen whispered. "This way lift it up with both hands—like this."

Solemnly the man smiled and nodded, his wildness ceasing, and kneeling in the new snow he tenderly lifted up a great double handful and held it as a priest holds up the Host.

Stephen left him and wondered what he could do with all this new and healthy freedom, and thought was child of wish for then he saw the ruined empty mill again covered with powdered snow, the stream a taut black bootlace round its strong back, the mighty shaft a slender, cold white finger, lifeless and forever spent.

And then he knew that this was the view of the Old Mill his youth had dreamed and known beyond any knowing. Age and youth had always wanted it with freedom. Looking down, he called softly and waited for the hollow clear-cut echo, but all was silent.

And the well he saw again, unchanged, the ice-cold water warmer now than winter's air, a still mirrorless eye. As if from behind and through the glass he saw the sun, the hub of Time's great wheel tirelessly spinning night and day, dusk, dawn, noon, midnight, high spring. . . .

"Spring, yes!" He smiled, seeming slowly to sink down into the dark water and seeing the hopeful spears of daffodils piercing the snow's white plain.

# *The Monocrats*

AT FOUR, THE morning after M'Adam's accident, Dulcie
knocks on James's door. Her weightless knuckles only
make a momentary dent in his heavy sleeping, and when
he starts to snore again she slips inside to wake him.

In the sun's rising he sprawls on the bed, ithyphallic on
account of a full bladder, the nightshirt hiked up around
his waist. As though floating in the long faded winceyette
nightgown, she gazes down on him, vaguely regretful for
having to break his troubled slumber. Apprehensively and
still not awake herself, her right thumb moves softly
across the tips of its fingers: the long night and its dream,
a flaming pillar. She had cried out as wheat poured from
it in molten streams.

James is rioting before her, and with a maternal shudder
of involuntary pity she watches his seed spurt and spurt
again and fall on his hairy barren thighs. Neither embarrassed nor ashamed, she feels offense by her own witness: such an open waste of something that should occur
within the mutual secrecy of passion's intimacy. Curiously,
tentatively, she touches with an index finger a blob of the
pallid manstuff, sensing its quick chill.

One infinitesimal germ of it, sufficient, she thinks. One germ, one unseen half of life, seeking with mystic urge through the dark corridors of her body, the egg of life; one tiny spark, a babe: a toddler, adolescent, youth, even a young man, perhaps, like Hamish, redheaded, and full of fun and spitless rage to live and rule the soil season by season; strong, clean-limbed, vital, and beautiful; a young M'Adam!

A fig for her spinster's dream! Almost reverently she covers James with a flap of blanket before she shakes his shoulder. His eyes open as she goes softly from the room, and he is not sure if he has loved her in a dream or in reality, until he knows it was a dream, yet somehow is embarrassed.

In her room she dresses. She hears him blundering downstairs and out into the yard, calling: "Bo! Come bo! Come bo!" to the cattle waiting round the pasture gate, and she makes her hair. She smiles to herself in the mirror. Were she to ask him to give her a child, he would be outraged. His puritanical mind would soon deny itself, if only to despise her. He had taken her hand once in the barn and, flattered, she had laughed, hurting him. But she had not laughed at him, rather at herself, knowing he only desired her in the heat of the day.

When she told her father, old M'Adam shook his head. Nothing personal against the man, but James was a hireling, and James would always be a hireling whether he bossed six hundred acres or one square yard.

She knew her father was right, but she also knew that soon she would be unfruitful. The section would have no children, and she wanted to bear a child as the earth bore its crops, springtime seeding, sweetening unto harvest. Adoption was never the same thing.

She did not resent her father's rejection. James?—she had no actual liking for the man. He was close and unwarm with animals. He was greedy, critical, and unforgiving, as dirty-minded six days a week as Old Testament on Sundays; a man born with an iron spoon and unable to forget the metal's bitter taste. He often reminded her of an oriental by the way he always tried not to admit a mistake.

Yet he was a Welshman, a Celt like herself; she had heard her father's tales. She knew intimately of travail, of the tragic Celtic remnants. In one way James was the most Celtic of them all, who liked a pretty face and lissome body, who seldom looked beyond his passion, denying even lust when his eyes had failed to find beauty enough for richer ravishment.

She looks somberly at the smiling face of her brother in the photograph on her dresser, and even now she cannot understand how he could smile so gaily just ten short days before he died at Vimy—a mere boy. It was his task to marry and make children. . . .

As she lights the fire, upset in herself and uneasy, she dwells upon her father's accident. It affects her as if she herself were hurt and the homestead lamed and made insecure. She cannot remember him missing a day. M'Adam had worked on even before and after her mother's funeral and she knew it was his way of mourning, weaving his grief into labor and giving his sorrow to the land. . . .

James the Welshman comes in to separate the morning's

milk and asks if he has time to feed the calves and pigs. She says no, breakfast is ready.

With an anxiety he does not have to simulate he asks as he sits down: "How's the boss?"

"He has pulled his back bad," Dulcie answers quietly.

"Duw!"

Then they hear M'Adam laboring downstairs. James tightens in himself. The old man drags in on a stick, his forehead glistening.

"You should have stayed in bed, father!" she says, making his chair ready.

"I'm okay," he grunts. "Mornin, Rhys," he mutters to James.

"Mornin, boss," James returns, staring at him, but there is nothing hostile in the old man's demeanor.

M'Adam is worrying about the hay, saying he will call the CPR to get an extra hand.

James protests. He can carry the hay on his own; but M'Adam insists that it would take him all of five days. There are storms about.

After the meal James finishes his morning cigarette outside, not wanting to think. After he feeds the calves and pigs he harnesses up Prince and Nell and sets out for the hayfield.

On the open road the morning is windless, full of light, the sun storing its heat for noon and afternoon, the earth a flat and barren plate fused at the rims to the sky's blue abyss. The field is a fifty-acre slab of stubble like a sandspit wracked with sea-waste. Its raked combers of weathered clover depress him, and the vast weight of matter to be moved from one place to another by a single pair of hands seems like a judgment.

Without supervision a hireling has little will to work. He figures, when he marries Dulcie, the section can be sold for cash, and home they will sail to the mountains where no acre lies level, where skies are near with cloud and give peace to the eye. . . .

"Duw!" He sits on the rack, tears in his eyes, and sings through a great Welsh hymn, but the sound of his voice fills him with emptiness. His stomach tightens. M'Adam's mere mishap is a delay. Worse, it will bring in a stranger, and he, James, will now have to wait for fall. Almost enough to wish that M'Adam hadn't fallen off the high load after all when Prince had plunged ahead to the jab of the pitchfork.

The hired man on Walter's section had fallen off the tractor, and the wheels had passed neatly across his chest. Instead, M'Adam had struggled gamely to his feet, swearing loudly at his own laxity and suspecting nothing.

With a shrug James starts grudgingly to work. Like his mind and plans the hay is twisted up, rolled by the raking into loose heavy ropes, every forkful to be fought for. Resting frequently, he wrangles on, and by the day's end he has carried only three small loads, the third one left exposed on the rack in the yard.

At supper M'Adam tells him the CPR is sending a man out on the morrow and that the radio has reported the possibility of severe storms in the locality. After the evening chores he wants to show keen and pitch off the load but cuts Dulcie a supply of firewood instead, filling the box by her stove and hoping for a chance to talk to her now that the boss is not about.

Although it is almost dusk, she keeps on bottling, working quietly and tirelessly and seeming neither lonely nor bored. James cannot solve her animal uncomplainingness. She reminds him strongly of his foster mother Mrs. Lewis Lefren and the way she used to put a drop of piss from her big rose-decorated chamber pot into the calves' milk to keep the help from drinking it on the sly.

He wonders if Dulcie ever thinks about a man—about anything outside money and her chores. She must be hard on thirty-five. He wants to talk to her, to climb across the fence of her reserve; but she keep silent, listening to his random remarks and seldom answering. In one way he despises her as he did old Mrs. Lewis Lefren, who stalked slowly to the chapel every Sunday morning, the big silver-knobbed stick in her hand, making her help follow at a respectful distance and counting them inside at the church door.

In the shadowed kitchen Dulcie seems less plain, the folds of her skirt falling mysteriously over her big backside with great flesh-rolls proud on her thighs. But Dulcie makes him unable to flirt with her. He talks about crops and the Bible, and animals—anything, wondering what would happen if suddenly he tried to take her.

Unlike Bee, the barmaid in Askaig, she is too big and practical, too like Mrs. Lewis. He would feel awkward and embarrassed, foolish if she repulsed him; and then there was the boss, always the boss. "What the hell!" he thinks. "I can only be fired."

But he checks the impulse in favor of his six long years,

his secret mortgage with its mounting interest—mounting
till all the land is his and Dulcie along with it and to hell
with M'Adam! Once even the boss had said that the man
who married Dulcie married the section.

Next morning after breakfast he stands again on the
back porch, staring dully at the not-yet-unloaded rack
of hay and beginning to wonder what the new man will
be like. He will only stay a few months, he tells himself,
and drift on again. The snow will come and the work
ease off: ice and the wind, twenty below and freeze a man;
and . . . long days with Dulcie! . . .

He sees now he should have waited but comforts himself. All will come right with patience, and, leisurely, he
unloads the rack. It takes him the most of an hour, the
sun out five, and the yard is shimmering. As he drives
down the parched road he sees in the northwest what
could be the gathering darkness of a storm.

In the hayfield he takes it easy, the ungathered fodder
no longer depressing him. Tomorrow will have help:
some wheezy old-timer or dumb Pole. Always the way.

Distant thunder draws his eyes to darkening cabbage-
heads of cloud. They are swelling fast and higher than he
thought, and before the approaching storm a pair of buz-
zards ride lazily on what breeze there is.

Absently he watches the birds wheel slowly nearer. The
air about him is almost totally still now. The hayfield is
a furnace, useless to continue loading. It would be wise to
go home, but he would look foolish going into the yard
with an empty rack if the cloud did not cross over.

Rolling a cigarette, he waits, nervous and uncertain,
watching the storm's intent. It stirs a tremor of atavistic

fear in him. He feels alone on earth, deserted, sacrificed to the sky's omnipotence. He moves closer to the horses for company.

Then the new wind comes in like laughter, smelling faintly of rain-sweetness, whispering, and toying with straws in small whirlpools. The overhanging nimbus cloud is now huge as war. Swiftly, loudly, the wind rises, and the thunder rolls suddenly above. The horses are snorting and restive, and he has left it too late to get back on the road.

Clambering onto the rack, he shouts at the beasts. Swiftly the wind follows, byrring and gustering so strongly that it lifts whole heavy ropes of hay and dances them like entwined snakes, driving them past him and scaring the horses.

Then the overture's crescendo dies into a calm that is uncanny. A single roll of thunder's timpani and abruptly the sun's light is smothered under a deep green gloom and in the pause, after a few warnings drops, the rain falls, filling the air so full of water he cannot see the horses' heads. They try to run, and he hauls back upon them hard, shouting hysterically "Steady steady steady" although he cannot hear himself.

With the snick of a wet whiplash lightning whirs before his face, and gasping against his panic he tries to steady the plunging animals, knowing he should stop them somehow and get down and take their heads. He urges them on instead, forcing them to wallow to their hocks in mud.

At last he comes to the road. The ditch to it is three feet deep and now black water. The horses plunge through it straight up the bank, but they cannot take the rack with them, their unshod hooves squelching and furrowing the marshed soil, their great haunches wrinkling and rippling with strain. Instinctively, they move to the left to go diagonally. His reins are too long, and before he can shorten them, Prince gets a forefoot on the road, pulling Nell with him and canting the rack at a crazy angle.

Sensing it lifting, he flings himself over the fore-rail to stand on the pole-step behind the horses, his terror now as frenzied as the storm. He feels the rack body turning over behind him and locks his fists in the horses' tails. Freed of the weight, the animals surge forward, stretching out in full gallop. The sulky-light wheels are blurs of spinning water and mud beside him, as they hurtle through the tempest.

The crossroads, he thinks: he must stop them or they will take the turn full tilt. Stiffened by greater hazard, he saws, straightens and takes the reins, hauling back so hard they open their jaws against the pain. They shake their heads and lose headway, the rain easing off to a sullen shower as the storm-heart beats down the southwest. They take the crossroads in a jolting walk.

"Hi-eee!" a voice hails. "Where's your wagon?"

He gasps in surprise and peers wildly through the rain. A tall, drenched figure with a small valise in hand is standing on the road verge, his suit clinging to him like a bathing costume and the rain rivering off his hatbrim.

"I'm looking for the M'Adam homestead." The stranger challenges, and James stiffens, resenting his critical glance toward the blowing horses. It seems as though the lanky stranger is burning himself for ever into his mind, a rugged, sunburned face with eyes dark as the storm's breast, pleasant all the same. Too pleasant, and James's storm-fear proceeds to coil itself into a tight knot in his stomach!

"It's bin a helluva storm," the stranger persists, sizing up his thickset, round-shouldered adversary.

"I work for M'Adam. You're the new man?" James mutters. With a back of a hand he wipes aside the long black hair stuck to his sloping forehead.

"Yep. Name's Moore," the stranger says with a quick smile. "Ye're not Irish, are ye?"

"No. Welsh," says James, stiffly. As though he does not want to tell Moore anything, he adds, "My name's James."

"Sure there's only a few mile of water between us," Moore grins, climbing up behind him asking: "What sort of place is it?"

"Not bad—quiet." Already James is trying to evaluate the Irishman's effect on the section and its emotional climate. His foot slips off the wet pole, and effortlessly Moore lifts him upright with his left hand, moving his hundred and seventy pounds as if he were a child.

When Moore jumps down to open the yard gate, he stands beside the still-nervous beasts' heads, examining them, noting the gelding's tender bit-bruised mouth and where the animal has gashed itself on a hind fetlock. James unhitches Nell and goes round Moore to free Prince.

"Ye musta bin pushin them?" says Moore.

James stops, startled: "Storm scared them. They tried to bolt. I could ardly hold the bastards, man!" He wants to tell Moore to mind his own business, but the Irishman's knowledgeable solicitude for animals unnerves him and deprives him of seniority. "Christ's sake don't say anything to the old man. He thinks more of is bloody horses than is men."

"Not a bad fault," Moore says, with a shrug, "but ye'd better see to that cut on the gelding's fetlock?"

"What cut?" James asks, nervously, his eye following the direction of Moore's hand.

As he frees Prince he looks up along the horse's steaming barrel, seeing Moore's left hand lightly on the bridle, and obeying the same irresponsible impulse as when he had pricked the horse and caused M'Adam's fall, he nips with extempore savagery the tender skin of the animal's sheath.

Prince plunges forward but is instantaneously checked and thrust back on his hocks by Moore who mutters soothingly: "Whoa, me boy! Whoa, me fine laddie!"

James leads the horses away and glances slyly over to the house. Dulcie is standing on the back porch. He tries to measure the extent of her possible witness.

She is bottling when they go into the house. Moore takes off his hat. His hair is sandy fair. James cannot guess his age.

"Mornin, ma'am," he greets Dulcie. "I'm from the CPR. My name's Moore—Cassidy Moore an I don't suppose I have to tell ye I'm Irish."

With a slight movement of her head Dulcie lets her big eyes rest upon his form, remarking the clinging wetness of his clothes.

Then James sees her make the first truly feminine gesture he has ever seen her make.

Her hand touches the V of her shirt neck and fiddles

with a button before she turns suddenly and goes into the parlor for her father.

"I'm M'Adam," the boss says in his thin strong voice. He has to come in slowly, Dulcie close behind him, ready to lend a hand.

Moore stares back as if he were here to buy the place. "Like I told the missus, I'm Moore—Cassidy Moore, Mr. M'Adam."

"She's my daughter," the old man corrects, shuffling over to his chair.

"I'm sorry, Miss M'Adam. But sure even with the stick your father looks fresh as thirty!"

Dulcie smiles with a furtive swiftness as her father grumbles: "Don't feel like thirty any more, Moore."

They talk. M'Adam explains his accident. Moore says he is thirty-six and has worked on farms for fifteen years. He is not long out of hospital with a knife wound and that is why he is idle.

"A crazy spick nearly finished me," he says. He opens his shirt and exposes a vicious red-lipped scar beaded evenly with white stitch marks. James watches Dulcie staring at the wound, while M'Adam, obviously taken with the man, smiles and starts explaining about the job which will end after the fall plowing. Moore says this suits him since he plans to go home for a winter's holiday, but he must go change into his work clothes. When he returns, he asks Dulcie if he may dry his suit at her fire. Without a word she takes the suit from him, which later James will notice on Moore's bed, all neatly pressed. After lunch they go to the hayfield to reassemble the rack, and

Moore looks in disapproval at the long hoof-gouges on the bank.

"You're lucky the whole outfit didn't go over."

James colors and fusses bossily around the rack, trying to assume his senior status. Moore talks away about Canada and fighting, working, loving, and drinking from Halifax to Vancouver. James listens avidly but jealously. The Irishman has done so much, while he has done little but stay in one place and work. Sadly, Moore confesses he should keep off the beer.

"It always gets me into trouble. Never affects me legs an fists, indeed. Always me head, an then I feel terrible afterwards. In the hospital they told me I'm what they call allergic. The blessed stuff it sorta poisons me. I'm goin to leave it alone even if it kills me the other way!"

As they start the chores after supper, Moore comments thoughtfully: "That Miss M'Adam, she's a queer sort of girl."

"In what way?" James asks.

"Well, I've traveled far an seen many women in and out of a bed but never have I seen one quite so plain."

"Aye," James chuckles, unexpectedly relieved. "She's no beauty, by God!"

"No!" Moore protests. "I don't mean it like that! Maybe you're sorta used to her, but if she was dressed up for a ball men'd be gazin at her. In her own way she's damn near good-lookin. How, I don't know."

James has never seen it like this and thinks over it as he milks. It makes him insecure again but not jealous since he wants the section and not the woman.

As the farm's slow and heavy rhythm takes hold, Moore

settles down and talks less and seems to enjoy the work. He is full of careless tireless strength. He cheers the place up. M'Adam is less frustrated and less surly, and Dulcie seems smarter in herself. The hay is gathered, and in the quiet days of the ripening grain the boss gets neglected jobs done. Moore's pace is much faster than M'Adam's, and James is dead-beat every evening trying to keep along with him.

At the end of the first week they are forking muck into the racks behind the stable. The Welshman suggests they visit Askaig for a few beers. Moore refuses, confessing to the pull, but he wants to settle in and keep off the beer. Curious how he is thinking now about Dulcie.

James sees his opportunity to mention the girl sarcastically.

"Agh she's all right, man," says Moore. "These farm women have the dull life."

"Do you know, Cass," James confides, "she hates your guts."

"Now why?" Moore asks, his face falling. "What have I done? What does she be saying, Rhys?"

"Never says much, that one," James mutters darkly. "But I know b'what she doesn't say."

"That's strange. I'd have said be the way she acts toward yourself she didn't care a damn if ye went or stayed."

"Arglwydd! She's always like that! She's a ploody man-hater she is!" James scorns, but his fierce glance is lost upon Moore's innocence.

"No, Rhys me boy, you're a poor judge of women. She's not a flier but she's no man-hater. She's quiet be her nature."

"She's a bitter tight ould maid, man!"

"Well, they do say ould fiddles have sweet airs!" Moore laughs. "By God, she has the fine big body! Bein quiet is no great fault in a woman."

"Iesu Mawr!" James challenges. "If y'want her y'can ave her!"

"Aye—aye," Moore says. "Indeed, I might try. I've often threw me cap at worse."

"What do y'mean?"

"Well, I wouldn't be trespassin on your ground, would I?" Moore asks seriously.

James laughs out loud to hide his anger, wishing he had never brought up Dulcie's name at all.

"What are y'after?" he jibes. "The section or Dulcie?"

"I hadn't been thinkin about the section, although it could be handy enough," Moore replies, looking closely at the Welshman.

"Iesu Grist, you're crazy, man! She doesn't want a man!" says James, trying to hide his uneasiness.

"Maybe she never had one?" Moore suggests.

James wants to tell him to keep away from Dulcie but cannot on top of what he has said against her. All the envy which he has been reconciling by the Irishman's eventual departure in the fall now reclaims him.

As they talk, they have built a full load on the rack, its smaller front wheels bedding in against a slight rise in the ground. Moore is using M'Adam's team, Jack and Jill, the two best horses on the section. With intentional carelessness James clouts Jack on the rump with the back of his fork and the beasts lunge forward and burst the traces. Shouting a loud "Whoa!" Moore runs to their heads, turning them round so he can say softly to James, "You're too goddamned free with that fork of yours."

James stares at him, wanting to bluster, but giving in. The connection between forks and plunging horses is yet so tender in his mind that he cannot even score against Moore by informing the boss of the mishap. One thing alone is certain: the Irishman has suddenly appeared as a greater threat even than M'Adam to his plans, and once again James's spider's mind starts spinning spiderwebs.

That same evening when Moore is yarning with M'Adam in the parlor, he hangs about the back porch until Dulcie comes out. She always comes outside at this time. She has powder on her body and no longer smells of her slightly musky personal odor.

In the leaden dusk of evening and its lintel of long cloud, he can hardly see her. She could be any female. The powder makes him think of Bee in the shadow behind Charlie's place. The swift association of images tightens his throat as he calls, "Dulcie? Dulcie?" He sees her now as a cross between Bee and Moore's estimation of her potentialities.

"What?" she asks flatly, stopping and halfway toward him.

He realizes for a woman she is tall. He is five feet ten, and her face is level with his own. More than ever he cannot think what to say to her, wanting to say, "Marry me, Dulcie, before that sonofabitch Moore asks you." He might take her rough hand, of course, but there again she might laugh at him. He might put his arms round her and say with honesty, "Dulcie, I want. . . ."

"What do you want?" she asks with an inflection of impatience.

He tries to ask her if Moore has made any difference, but he realizes how little there is to be made different. His throat moves, he licks his lips, but he makes no sound. His inability to say anything at all fills him with further rage against her.

Presently, the screen door flapping behind her with its small song of drowsy flies tells him she has gone. Her faint perfume is all that is left with him, and lonely and disconsolate, he sits on the edge of the porch, knowing now that all men are his adversaries, pitying himself.

He tries to imagine Dulcie's body as Moore sees it, his sense of loss accentuating its appeal, and he goes to bed full of angry desire. By and by Moore climbs the stairs, and he hates the Irishman afresh, as though he had disturbed a love act.

Moore come in and turns up the lamp, yawning and unbelting his jeans, and pushing jeans, pants, shoes and socks off in one operation as he talks endlessly about M'Adam. The boss must have been a hell of a man in his early days. Imagine starting a quarter section on a few bucks and a mortgage and putting up all the buildings with only his wife to help! A shame to have lost his son and then his wife!—but he still kept going!

"He say Canada's goin to be the center of the world. Soon. No, it has all a nation needs, Rhys. He showed me articles the newspapers have published about soil erosion, says Canadians may wake up to find themselves a great nation but without fertility. Have ye ever read any of them books of his on agriculture?"

James grunts, pretending drowsiness. In all six years M'Adam has seldom discussed anything with *him* outside of farm jobs. Moore reaches under the bed for the enamel chamber pot, James watching him from beneath his eyelids, seeing his long smooth thighs. Is that what Dulcie saw in him, that first day after the rain?

Moore is saying, "Aye, an Dulcie's not so dumb as ye might think. The old man has educated her to think for herself." His lust undead, James senses it transmute itself into a powerful pointless hate, more blundering than lust and timed to gentle rhythm: *I will get this Irish bastard Moore. I will get this goddamned Moore,* as if Moore were lust's object and his own dark hate an amulet.

Sunday is the next day. Moore and he do the morning chores together and lie in the sun until dinner, James reading his Bible, and sometimes bursting forth with snatches of a hymn.

In the afternoon James sees Dulcie in a white and pink frock stepping off the front porch and going through the five-acre windbreak. He gets up to follow, but Moore is in the yard. It is Moore who vaults the fence to head her off. Not far along they stop and talk, and James creeps near to overhear.

". . . wonderin what you've got agin me, Miss M'Adam?" Dulcie looks at her hands and says nothing.

"I guess I'm only a hired man," Moore says softly. "You're a big farmer's daughter, but I'm a farmer's son an I've saved five thousand dollars an I sorta like the looks of ye."

"Me?" Dulcie asks. She laughs shyly and turns away.

Moore beckons, and as she approaches uncertainly, he leans toward her; picking her up swiftly and lifting her high and clean. Once again James is shocked at the smoothness of his strength. Moore sets her down lightly and she stands facing him without movement.

"Miss M'Adam—Dulcie," he says softly. "Ye have a heart like a little girl."

She does not look into his face. Her eyes are on the scorched hollow in his throat below the Adam's apple.

"I've had plenty to do with wimmen in me time. . . ."

She puts a finger to her lips, not wanting him to talk. She does not need to talk. He does not have to sell himself, and now she must wait until conventions are satisfied and he asks her to marry him. She wants to tell him, but they return slowly to the house.

That evening when Moore talks to the old man and James catches Dulcie in the back kitchen, "You watch out for that Moore!" he says. He has his Bible under his arm, and he snatches it into his left hand and pounds it with his right. "The Book tells you!" Impassively she listens, holding her hands together, not moving away.

"Moore's no more'n a wild drunken sot, Dulcie! He can't resist no woman!"

"Christ's ancestors were not blameless, James," she says quietly, and James sees the curved bows of her thigh muscles and her skirt folding in a little valley between them and hastily puts the Bible back under an arm. Moore said she was like a little girl.

"He's only passing the time with you," he says, more boldly now. "If y'heard some of the things he says?"

"What about?" she demands. He swallows. "He's fornicated with dozens of wimmen, he has! Bad wimmen, Dulcie."

"Better experience than hole-and-corner chastity."

"He'll make a whore out of you, Dulcie!"

"Takes two of us to do that."

"But I've known your father an you a *long time,* Dulcie!"

"The same length of time we've known you."

"Of course, it's never what a man has done nor even what he is but . . ."

"It's what he *might* be, James!"

"Moore'll never be any different!"—defiant, but the challenge of her silence is unnerving. "Sure. Sure," he mutters. She is too smart with words for him, like old M'Adam with his book learning.

"Are you so certain Moore won't?" she asks with a slow small smile.

"Don't laugh at me, Dulcie," he says. "Now don't you laugh!"

"But I'm not laughing at you, James, I'm laughing at what you're tryin to do."

"An what *am* I tryin to do?"

"You know," she says and goes upstairs.

So he sits down abruptly at the kitchen table, drumming his fingers on his Bible, hearing her moving about above him as she goes to bed; and for the first time in his life he hears her singing.

Next week James prepares and discards a dozen plans. He could get rid of Moore in several different ways but cannot be completely sure of avoiding retribution. And now he regrets his words with Dulcie on the subject of the Irishman. Every time he sees M'Adam now, he tries to divine a change in the old man's attitude. Finding none, he creates one, sentencing himself, James, to dismissal instead of Moore after the fall plowing; and all that is left for him to build upon with safety is one remote and idle chance—the Irishman's confessed weakness for beer. However, he begins to question Moore who readily admits that after a few pints he cannot remember much.

"What did y'say the doctor called it, Cass?"

"A kind of alcoholic amnesia."

"What hell's that, man?" James asks.

"It's like being punch-drunk," Moore explains.

"An what's that?"

"Where hell have ye bin?" says Moore, laughing. "Don't y'know what slaphappy is?"

Envious anyway of the Irishman's experience, James deeply resents the implication of inexperience behind Moore's words. He explains that while the narrower road he endeavors to walk may offer less excitement than the broad and busy one on which Moore swaggers, it is humility in life that counts. In the back of his mind James gratefully accepts the weapon which Moore has innocently offered, and he works on the Irishman about going to Askaig. He describes Charlie Peace's place and Saturday nights in lurid terms. He paints the picture of a boom town in the gold-rush days, while in reality the hamlet is dull and lawful. Its constable is rigorous, and Charlie has to keep his place superficially clean. Any public interference with his two serving girls is sure to earn a summary ejection.

Moore listens with increasing interest, and once again his heart and mind begin to sense the oppressiveness of a constructive and planned security, and the Welshman perceives a glimmer of success. By now James has completely identified himself with the role of protector and secret policeman to the M'Adams and their section, justifying his actions more and more as a moral process duly sanctioned by his God. But apart from James the Welshman's portrayals of carnival at Askaig, Moore the Irishman wants to buy a shirt and jeans.

On the Saturday Dulcie is working in the garden. She watches them saddle the horses and ride off into the smoke-blue coolness of evening, two small black figures etched upon the sun's somber disk. A moon thin as a filigree of silver beholds the fading world, and the sun swiftly sinks into a darkness of length and breadth immeasurable.

Evening is Dulcie's best and most peaceful time. Her chores are finished for the day, and night is a charitable and loving stranger come to her door.

On countless evenings at this time she has worked in the garden for relief or stood a little while on the back porch to watch the stars wash big and bright across the sky.

No longer able to see weed apart from plant she pushes her splayed hands down like roots into the warm moist earth, turning her head toward the big barn's brooding shadow. Her father and mother lived first in the barn and begot her there before the house was built. How sweetly the crickets sing, their thousand cries a sigh upon the universe. She rises, and as she carries the spade and fork slowly over to the barn, she thinks about Moore and the burning pyre that was her dream: James and Moore, one, a blackened glass, the other, instant and clean as a struck match.

The barn is a dark warmness, the Tammuz moon now tarnished with haze. Obeying an impulse, she goes carefully over to a bin of wheat beside the yawning door, and combs through the kernels with her fingers.

## 2

As they ride into Askaig, James harps on beer and the two café girls. He describes minutely the intimacies that he has had with Bee.

Moore recalls a blonde called Bee whom he had known ten or so years before. In the fall it was. She was a maid in a hotel, and he had his pockets full of spring and summer wages. She had started by helping him spend his bank roll and finished by claiming he had given her a child. Later she had written him for fifty dollars to pay an abortionist, but he had no more money.

Alarmed that Moore isn't entering into the spirit of things, James boasts about his buddy, Charlie Peace. "Always serves me double helpings, Cass, and that's a fact. Burns incense every morning at an idol. Calls the girls geisha number one and two, sleeps with both of them, three to the bed!"

"Sounds like a real heathen!" Moore laughs.

"Sure. He's a Jap. But don't ever tangle with him, Cass.

He may be fat—he can still bounce like a baby the biggest bohunk in the province."

Moore whistles appreciatively.

"But Charlie's a regular fellow. He likes his fun. The girls, too. I've seen customers sample their legs at the tables!"

When they stable the horses, Moore reluctantly agrees to a social drink in the beer parlor, but James keeps on ordering, and the Irishman begins to lose count when he passes the fifth half-pint. Then they yaw about the town until an irate farmer threatens to have them run in for trying to make his wife. The town constable appears and warns them to behave or else go home.

So far, James is disappointed. Moore still manifests mere wild good humor. When they look in on the small dance hall, the Welshman starts a row with a big guy whom Moore hits for him. After they are both slung out, the Welshman realizes that Moore at last has become coldly absently berserk. He heads for Charlie Peace's place.

The café is full of hired men and a few farmers' families. The two bleached washy blondes are busy. The room is stuffy and warm, so neither of them wear much more than light white cotton overalls and pants; and the heads of the hired men turn in unison, their eyes following the flop and bounce of breast.

One of the girls comes over to take their orders. James kicks Moore beneath the table. "Hello, Bee!" he says with a leer.

She mutters "Hello" and stares at Moore.

"Hello, Bee," he says, like a caress.

Charlie sets some orders on the counter, and James gets

up and swaggers over to him. Charlie nods with a quick smile. "How'ya, Jamiee. You not come last week, heh?"

In full view Moore has placed a hand on Bee's rump. The hired men smile, and a farmer's wife tries to talk her two children's eyes away. Bee whispers a warning and moves; but Moore smiles, and his fingers bite into the loose flesh. She glances round and sees Charlie staring at them and says in a louder voice: "Take your hand offa me, y'big heel!"

Moore laughs lazily and keeps his hand where it is and then Bee picks up a cellar of salt and slings it into his face, dodging away from his hand as Charlie lifts the counter flap and waddles swiftly down to them. He is a short, fat, and very broad-shouldered little man around fifty and wears a white sweat-wet shirt and white duck pants with a red belt that bites into his belly.

Moore barely sees him through a haze of rage and lifts him off the ground. Then, somehow, he cannot get rid of him. For a few seconds there is a stiff struggle, until the Irishman is thrown. Charlie chops him with the side of his hand and Moore goes limp. James immediately joins in and helps Charlie drag him outside.

Quite rational and unmoved, Charlie apologizes to James for his violence, and James guarantees that he will look after Moore. Then the town constable reappears and gives them fifteen minutes to get out of town.

When Moore comes round, he cannot remember anything, but under the delusion that he is protecting James, he is willing to fight anything on two or four legs. His eyes are wide and staring. Their animal vacuity scares the Welshman, who instinctively recoils from the automaton he has helped create. He realizes that he must somehow abandon Moore to find his own inevitable trouble if he is to see Bee before he starts for home. The constable returns again, assessing the extent of the Irishman's inebriation with a practiced eye.

"Get him outa here!" he says, and James obeys, muttering something about the horses.

He steers Moore round to the railroad tracks directly behind Charlie's place. They lean against a boxcar watching the bright rectangle of the café's back door. Moore keeps mumbling about a woman. James quiets him, saying he will find a dame for both of them, the beer having dulled the conscious edge of his spite, while whetting the point of his lust.

"Wait here, man, till I see what's goin on," he advises as one of the girls slips out of the café door.

He goes over. It is Bee. She is obliging a customer in the vegetable shed and does not take long. James hails her as she goes inside again, stuffing her dollar down between her breasts.

"How are ya, Jamie," she says, sidling over, no longer a drab waitress but wholly free and female. "Where's the big wise guy?" she murmurs, looking past him.

"Back there," he mutters. He cannot see her very well, but her perfume arouses him. He sways contentedly on his feet.

Still peering through the darkness Bee says, "Mister Moore's a hell of a man."

"Do y'know him?" says James uneasily.

"Used to. Way back, the dirty dog!"

James's thoughts are beginning to reek and reel, the

alcohol loosening his reason and releasing primitive doubts. Her interest for Moore fills him with impatience. On impulse, he leans toward Bee like a child, resting his forehead on her shoulder.

But she talks on about Moore. "Where does he work?" she says. She cannot seem to understand his pain, and suddenly he sees her as the single being responsible for his entire despair—Bee, Dulcie, Moore, M'Adam. She is become a further outrage to his past, and in her denial of him once again, James begins to hate. *Wanton woman! Takes men as a newspaper takes reading! For a dollar!*

He sees her as his eternal enemy, wants to grip the pale column that is her throat and expunge Moore forever from her consciousness, as if through her he could also bring down Moore. It could have ended there in ritual sacrifice. Instead, he grasps her forearms, pulling her roughly against him.

She does not resist, still seeming to peer into the shadows and absently, by force of habit, she starts her small love play. Her giving body, her sweet smell, her hair moving on his cheek: for a few moments he forgets everything but the possession of her, but it is neither respite nor release. His jealousy is more virulent still and now takes further hold. It is Moore, not him the girl has mated!

With as much violence as he had grasped her, he shoves her from him, and Charlie Peace comes to the door and peers out blinking. She comes quickly back so that Charlie will not notice and catches hold of James's coat. "What about my buck, Jamie?" she whispers.

Tugging his coat away from her he laughs out loud, "Like the ploody June thrush, ye've had your buck!"

"Come on!" she hisses, grasping him again and looking round anxiously at Charlie.

"Go to hell!" says James. Grasping her wrist, he spins her away from him, and moves nonchalantly into the wedge of light from the café.

"Oh, it's you, Jamiee," Charlie says, relieved.

"How ya, Charlie! Duw, I'm sorry for the trouble. I never knew the damn fool'd act up like that, man!"

Charlie nods his head several times. "I didn't hurt him ver much—noh?"

"Nah! He's tough as wire. He asked for it, Charlie!"

"Mebbie. He a little dronk. I want no trouble, Jamiee," Charlie mutters, rubbing his small fat hands together as if they were chill. "Trouble no good."

"Iesu Grist!" says James. "Y'can handle em, Charlie! Moore's a tough hombre!"

"Yeah!" Charlie nods unhappily. "He ver strong. Jamiee —you keep him away from me, yes?"

"You're not scared of him?"—laughing.

"Noh. I scared nothink, Jamiee. You don't understan. I am what you call judo man. Mebbie I kill Moore—"

James's throat tightens. Forcing himself to appear indifferent, he asks Charlie more questions. They talk, and he forgets all about Bee who stands waiting in the shadows behind them. Someone calls Charlie from inside, and James goes back to Moore. Bee follows softly behind him. Moore is standing patiently by the boxcar like a dog that has been ordered to wait.

"Just been talking to your friend, Charlie," says James.

The next thing that Bee sees is Moore, moving fast toward the café. She runs over and tries to stop him, but he does not even recognize her. Brushing her aside, he kicks open the door. Charlie pokes his head out and walks into a fist. As he leans back against the boxcar, James sees a grotesque fight, heaving back and forth across the lighted doorway. There is a thud as a body hits a wall, and silence, until he hears Bee's scream. "God! You've killed him!"

Swiftly James dodges round to the street, making for the horses. With spastic fingers he tightens the girth strap and puts the bit in the mouth of the first, then mounts, leading the other animal down the street.

A crowd is gathering outside the café and the constable pushes through it, and then a voice shouts: "Fire!"

The word flashes across town, emptying houses, store, dance hall and beer parlor into the street. A bell clangs hysterically, and someone beats the big wrought-iron wheel-shoe that hangs on a gibbet in front of the store. No one knows where the fire is.

Then it declares itself, and James pulls the horse up short. It leaps from the side of a tall grain elevator, searing with its blood light the upturned faces of the crowd.

James blinks, the suddenness of the light discovering him, for he is between them and the fire. It seems to lay him bare before them all. And when the momentary shock is gone he accepts this stern sign of blame and condemnation with proper Celtic awe and reverence. The fire is a pyre for Moore and its lurid light the flaming ascendency of his departing soul.

"What caused it?" he calls to an old man.

"Rain, son," is the answer.

"Rain an—an fire? . . ."

"Off the storms. Corn heats up. Seen it happen a dozen times before."

James shudders, seeing again the tall wet form of Moore standing in the road: "Where's your wagon?"

He heels his horse fiercely, jumping it, and thunders from the fire. The lead rein checks his left hand hard, and he knows it is Moore holding him back. He plunges through the crowd, scattering the people as he heads for home trying to make the horses run, but the animal on the lead rein will only trot. He does not look back till he has passed halfway, and the fire is a dark red heart on the horizon.

M'Adam shouts for his daughter, the abnormal light in his room making him nervous for his homestead. Dulcie goes to him, looking out his window, saying that the fire is far away in the direction of Askaig.

"Must be big," he says. "Could be an elevator."

Then Dulcie remembers her dream. The light's malevolence moves the night like a false sunstart, and while the trees stand stark and cowering against the glow, the whole land seems to breathe uneasily and long for the dawn. She puts her hand on her heart, feeling it beating through the flesh of her breast.

James is too weary to think of anything but bed and sleep. He puts the horses out to pasture, leaving their bridles and saddles by the gate. He removes his shoes on the back porch, creeps to his room, and falls into bed to sleep better than he has slept in weeks.

It is five o'clock when James awakens. Invigorated, he stands awhile at his window, gazing out on the dew-bejeweled yard. Beyond, he sees the tall lances of green corn glittering in the sun, and notes with satisfaction how near they are to ripening and harvest. Confident once more, he whistles through his chores. When he comes in to separate the milk, he treats himself, as he was wont to do before Moore's arrival, to a cupful of warm nutty cream.

As he sits down at the table, Dulcie asks him where Moore is. James knows she is thinking that the Irishman is sleeping it off.

He stirs the milk deliberately into his porridge.

"Where is he?" she says again, stridently this time.

He stops his stirring with reluctance. "I've bad news, Dulcie," he says.

"What news?" she quickly asks.

He shrugs. "I told you Moore was no good, Dulcie."

"Has he gone? What's he done?"

"Yep," he nods.

"Tell me!"

"He gotta few beers an cut loose. Duw Mawr! The man was mad, Dulcie!"

"Where? Where is he now?" Her eyes are black as coals upon him, and he has to look away.

"He's dead, Dulcie," he says in a whisper. He hears her chair move sharply back, and she goes upstairs to tell her father. Immediately the old man shouts for James.

"Why couldn't y'help?" she asks when the tale is told.

James shrugs helplessly and glances at M'Adam. "Iesu, Dulcie! He was a goliath!" is all that he can say.

When feeding the skim to the calves, he sees her catching Joy the light mare in the pasture and calls to her. She does not answer, and he watches her drive off in the buggy.

For the first time he considers the possibility that Moore

might not be dead, and he wanders listlessly about until she returns. She rubs down the sweating mare in the stable. He offers to take over, but again she does not answer. He tries to discover something by her expression. She seems so quiet and unannoyed. His stomach turns in a wild surge of apprehension.

"Did you see Moore, Dulcie?" he has to ask.

She stops what she is doing and looks levelly at him, her big eyes wet and dead, and he knows for sure that Moore is dead. He can't help trembling with anticipation. The section is safe and free again.

When she goes to the oatbin, he follows.

"Dulcie?" he says.

She turns from the bin with a scoop of crushed oats in her hand.

"Dulcie?" he says again, placing his hands lightly on her elbows.

She stands quite still, looking down at the grain oats then looking up at him, past him, as Bee had looked, through him as if he were not there at all. For the first time he sees her as a woman, and basks in the bright warmth of her soul. Its healing light is a mask to her uncomeliness, which Moore had somehow sensed as he laid eyes on her so long ago. And in his new sight each limb and member of her strong body takes on beauty as he prepares to seal Moore's death for good and all.

She tries to move away, but he stays her, wanting to linger on the bright threshold of discovery. Her movement away from him stirs his desire, even as Bee in the dark had done before his fouling her.

He closes his hands on her arms and finds her body

rigid and unresponsive. To make her curve to him, he slips an arm across her back, and suddenly she hurls the oatmeal in his face. Half-blinded, he holds on, trying to wipe his eyes upon his arm. When he is able to see again, tears are running down her cheeks. Joy whimpers for her oats, and humbly he feels compelled to let her go, yet never has he desired a woman more fiercely than he does now.

Methodically, Dulcie lifts another scoopful from the bin, feeds the animal, and leaves, dropping the scoop by the door and dusting the loose oats off her frock, the same pink and white frock she wore in the wood with Moore last Sunday, two hundred years before.

They eat the Sunday meal without a word. James loiters round the yard. Then a car drives up at the gate and two RCMPs come across the yard, asking for the Welshman. He acknowledges his identity in a small scared voice. They ask questions but are not hostile and inform him he will be served with a summons to attend the inquest. After they go, he stands a long time in the yard.

Monday passes. Dulcie keeps to her bottling, and James receives the summons for the inquest on the following forenoon. Dulcie tells him she will go with him, and he is pleased.

Charlie Peace has briefed a lawyer. A second counsel acts for the witnesses. Charlie's man claims justifiable defense of life and property. Charlie has many friends, and the jurymen are mostly farmers not greatly sympathetic to hired men given to alcoholic outbursts.

Then Bee starts crying, interrupting the court and asking for a hearing. She explains that Charlie has threatened her if she says too much and tells about the conversation she overheard between her employer and James and how James got Moore going at the boxcar. She is incoherent, and Charlie's counsel jumps on her, but it comes out that the Japanese took fifty cents on every dollar that she and her colleague earned on the side. Charlie cannot produce an immigrant's documents. James is recalled and admits Charlie did say something or other but persists he did try to keep Moore away from trouble. The jurymen pull in their horns, and the coroner orders an adjournment and detains Charlie pending further investigations.

Throughout everything, Charlie has remained impassive and stares for a long time at James and then at Dulcie who is weeping quietly. She drives home in silence, and James gives up trying to talk to her. At the farm she leaves him to see to the mare, and when he comes into the house, the table is not laid for the meal. Dulcie stalks out of the parlor and throws a wad of bills on the table.

"There's your wages," she says, "with a month's pay ahead."

He laughs nervously, looking from the money to the girl. "Duw! Y'can't fire me just like that, Dulcie! An I'm not entitled to give you any reasons."

M'Adam drags himself into the kitchen saying, "This is what Dulcie wants, Rhys. She's the boss, an she'll quit if you don't."

Dulcie starts preparing a scrap meal, and James thinks it over. "When do y'want me to go, Dulcie?" he says.

"Soon as you can."

"But where'll I go?"

"Canada's a big place."

"The CPR'll get you another farm," M'Adam suggests helpfully. It is the homelessness in the man's voice.

"I can't get a train anywhere until tomorrow," says James, hopelessly.

"You can walk an you can buy a bed somewhere," Dulcie says.

"Agh, let him stay till tomorrow," M'Adam suggests. Dulcie shrugs.

By habit, James works round the yard in the afternoon. At six he watches Dulcie fetch out the milking pails and go up the pasture for the stock. He starts the pump engine for her and puts corn in the cows' mangers. The thirsty animals rush to jostle round the trough, horses and all. He sorts them out, and one by one the five milch cows satisfy themselves and walk slowly to their stable. But she acts as if he is not there and does all the chores well enough and separates the milk, running short of corn for the pigs and going into the barn for a fresh sack.

He sits on the edge of the back porch, smoking and watching and vaguely resenting her activity as an interference. Although he tells himself, as he stands up, that he is only going to help her carry the corn sack, as he comes through the barn doors his hands are moist and his knees are trembling. He looks around the barn's labyrinth where sunlight and shade lie together, his mind unconsciously enumerating the untidy contents as if he had not seen them before. Dulcie is stooping in a corner, filling a sack from a heap of crushed mixed grain which he and Moore had put through the hammer mill on Saturday morning. He had been talking about women, and the

Irishman had kept laughing, his face floured white like a clown.

He goes over to take the sack out of Dulcie's hand, but without looking up she says, "I don't want any help, James."

Feeling foolish, he stands and looks at her. She shakes down the sack and ties it, cutting the string with the old carving knife that lives in the barn. He notices the gentle starting of her breasts inside her shirt as she bends over. They fall forward sweetly, pushing out the loose shirt so he can see almost all of their tender shapes.

He feels sorry for her and close to her. If she would only have sense. What was it Moore said once?—something about in spite of what people think, bodies can find each other and be happy together. Something like that.

In a few seconds she will lift the sack and walk out and tomorrow will come. He must not let her go. As she puts both hands to the sack, he places a foot on it and she looks up, saying, "Take your foot off it."

The look on her face, behind her face, shocks him. It is the first time he has ever seen cold feminine revulsion. It forces him to admit to final failure and oddly he feels free. All his past envies and frustrations are suddenly become worthless and blow away to dust: and years and years that have not taken his manhood past the day when his mother shut the door for the last time and went down the road past Jones the Post, a flock of crows flying ahead of her across the valley.

"God damn Moore!" he mutters.

"Silent the dead," she says. "He'll haunt your miserable days. Now, get out of here!"

"Dulcie—" he whispers, a sob in his voice. "I was the man for you . . ."

"Mebbie," she says briskly and pulls the sack away, and then he knows he cannot leave without first humbling this plain, hard woman who still taunts him and offends. He knows she will, with fight and hate, sweeten lust as Bee could never with her easy giving. He smiles to himself, although his desire for her is much more subtle and fond, but since she is sending him away he cannot wait.

Reading his face and lifting the old knife, Dulcie warns, "Keep your hands off me!"

Knife, Dulcie, barn, homelessness, and Moore all drive him to his dream.

His hand leaps instantly to her wrist and twists. The knife falls, and he seizes, her, lifting her off her feet, burying his face against her to save his eyes. She is very strong, so he forces her back on a bin of loose wheat and she falls. The wheat cushions their tumbling, and there is only the sound of their gasping breath. He tries to pin her with his weight, but the slippery grain allows her to move under him. Her hands rip at his face, and he has to hold them. Once she bites his shoulder, but he does not feel it after the first scorch of pain.

"Let me, Dulcie," he whispers hoarsely, "or I'll kill you!" He shifts his hands quickly to her throat, making her cough, and suddenly she makes no resistance.

At first he thinks that she has fainted. Her eyes are closed, her face so small and white upon the wheat. Yet with a pagan gleam of triumph, thinking he has wooed and mastered, he kisses her cool lips. He wants to linger, but against his will he hastens. He rips open her shirt,

exposes the startlingly white thorax on which lie innocently the small mounds of her breasts. Touching them
first lightly, then grasping them so that she winces, "Iesu
Mawr!" he exclaims reverently.

But her quietude still puzzles and impedes him. It is
beyond lust, love, and any sexual motive, frighteningly
so; and he feels warned: stealing, he will lose all, while
to give way without reward is something that he cannot
comprehend. Not self-pity but pity for what he is himself
disturbs him, for though his act may be impure, such an
act it was that once begat a god. So he proceeds, as if he
*were* an animal and forced to mate without self-conscious
pleasure, while his devious mind remarks the Cinderella
softness of her body and its languid radiance. Only then
does he realize the extent of his failure, as if just now he
were no more than working off a binge that started perhaps in the beer parlor on a Saturday, or started when his
mother went away, or when Mrs. Lewis died and he had
left for Canada, or watched the ship's long surging wake
for hours on end and heard the screw going *bump bump
bump* like his own heart. For he is unable to love her
either, and all women are delegated in his mind to the
lot of the Bees of the world. Save as an animal, and with
a shudder of sorrow, he admits his impotence.

Only once she moves a little and groans against his passion, which she now receives, lifting her loins to him.
Swiftly, he spends himself against his will, and moves,
cursing himself for buying a mad moment at the expense
of a month's regret. But she holds him. Shyly, he looks at
her, and she is smiling, as if doting on a secret joke, and
he feels tricked.

"Duw Mawr, woman!" Thinking of Moore, he tears himself away, and still she smiles. With boyish curiosity, "You're not mad, Dulcie?" he asks.

"No," she answers absently. Getting to her knees in the wheat she gazes curiously at a few red-golden grains in her hand before she stands and shakes her clothes. Looking at him she says softly, "But if I have a child by you, James, I pray to God it won't be like its father. You're only a man because you're a male, and you're a hired one at that. Now git!"

"It may take more'n one, Dulcie . . ."

"No, but you hit me the right time."

"Iesu tirion!" he breathes. Why, she was near to laughing! As if reading his thoughts, she turns back to the sack and ignores him.

He puts a hand lightly on her arm. "Dulcie?" he says. "Dulcie? . . ."

She hefts the sack onto the crusher and pulls it on her back. Then she turns and stands there watching him.

"Dulcie . . ." he says, but he cannot finish. Scared of her now, he rushes off into the kitchen where the twelve-bore is and hides the box of shells.

The next morning she wakes him up at dawn, seeing him again as she had seen him before, and she looks down on him and wonders.

And against her will, which has tried to shut out Moore from any memory, she sees instead the fine lithe body of the Irishman, a man of her own who would come to her even in barn or stable or on the fields or in the night and take her swiftly or slowly and press her form with his weight so the earth would take its imprint of her like a seal.

Pursing her lips, she measures her hand over James's face and deals a stinging slap. "Come on, James," she says, "time you were gettin along."

He packs his few belongings and puts on his Sunday suit and shoes. Dulcie has a good breakfast for him and sits by quietly as he eats. Vainly, he tries to measure the stiffness of her resolve, making the meal last. She shifts and glances at the clock. "I got work to do," she says. "Finish an get moving."

Like a child he asks, "Do I have to go?"

She nods.

"Lemme stay, Dulcie?" he pleads with the tears in his eyes genuine enough since leaving the farm is now like leaving home.

She does not answer.

"But Moore was no damned good, Dulcie!" he protests.

"Maybe. Sometimes a woman likes a man because . . ."

"But look what I spared you! You only knew Moore a coupla days."

"And I'd have liked a chance to know him better."

"But he was a drunken whorin waster!" His voice is rising in his hopelessness. "He'd a gone through the section inside five year!"

"Father liked him. Have you finished eating yet?"

He stands up staring, wiping his mouth with the back of a hand, the dead unseeing light back in his eyes. She reaches over and takes a revolver from the table drawer.

"This was my brother's gun, James," she says, pointing it at him.

"Go on. Shoot me!" he jibes.

"I will, if necessary," she says. "Besides, you're only a hired man. Names. Understand?"

He nods slowly.

"Listen!" she says. "I've been adding up a whole lot of small things. Father has built loads for forty years an never once fell off. A child of three could handle any horse on the section. Do I go on?"

For a moment he watches her, and sees the hammer lift and her knuckle whiten on the trigger. Her eyes are dark and dull, and he knows that she will shoot.

He walks slowly down the drive and turns into the road, coming soon to the section's boundary. Already the homestead and its little cloud of windbreak trees is a miniature behind him. Before he leaves the section he takes up a handful of its earth. The feel of it makes him more cheerful, and he figures he will return in a few months when Dulcie has settled down.

He gets a lift into Askaig and boards the train, from which he looks out onto the blackened hulk of the burned-out elevator. The great mounds of wheat around it are like piles of gravel, charred and useless, and men are shoveling them into wagons.

The conductor calls faintly: "Goin . . . goin . . ." and the train begins to move. Already he feels easier. He will take a holiday, and he feels a thrill in setting out. There are only two hired men in the coach, both of them chewing snuff and spitting on the floor between their feet, while before him roll green endless deserts of grain.

He makes his way to the lavatory, and coming back,

meets Charlie Peace with a big RCMP behind him. The sudden appearance of the quiet little man dressed up in a blue suit embarrasses him. He does not know what to say. Charlie smiles, nodding his head and saying, "Hallo, Jamiee!"

As if surprised and pleased, James answers, "Howya, Charlie." Then glancing at the policeman and with a show of sympathy, "How's everything workin out?"

"Pretty good," the Japanese replies brightly, lifting a jocular finger and wagging it. "Mebbie you send me home, Jamiee? Yes, maybe to die! Somehow you get me bad trouble. Why? I always kind to you—yes?"

"Come on, Charlie," the policeman says.

"Okay, I go. Well, Jamiee, good-by. Good luck where you go, yes?"

He holds out a small short hand, and although James by some instinct does not want to touch it, he has to. As he puts his own right hand forward, he notices a little pellet of the section's soil still on his palm, and then the policeman shouts as the ground seems to leap away from him.

In one gigantic effort Charlie grunts, and James's body flies headfirst through a window, shattering the glass. The policeman grabs at Charlie, but the Japanese slips the hold and throws him. Then he waddles swiftly down the carriage aisle, leaning against the drag of the slowing train.

He opens a door and stands on the step as the train stops at the end of a trestle bridge over a deep eroded gully, and looks down, his eyes quietly indifferent to the untidy thing that is James's body seventy feet below. The policeman hurries up behind him. Charlie's face becomes very sad and solemn, and he leaps outward with a graceful movement like a bird flying or a fish swiming, his fat body spinning over and over as it falls.

# No Fatted Calf

"Bwrwrwrwrrr . . ." Adam Finney said.

He kept making this sound with a burl of his numb lips. It helped him stay within himself, for his life wanted to wander away from his body into the trackless night.

Except that now and again it pulled on the bit of rope in his left hand, he hardly knew the little black bitch was beside him. It was an unseen living thing, a vital movement in the darkness on the end of the lead like his own life in the darkness of his body. Sometimes he forgot about the dog and was startled when lightly it brushed his leg. The night was bone black. He could not even mark the trees against the drizzling wet fleece of the sky and only knew he was on the road by its hardness under his numb feet. Many times he wandered onto the verge, stopping and feeling for the road again with a blind man's foot.

Frequently the dog crossed the rope over his shins, and he chucked the beast back with an impatient curse. He did not want her, and had he thought about it, he might well have loosed her. Sometimes a straggling brier clawed his legs, but he chucked at the dog all the same, blaming the innocent animal for his general predicament.

"Bwrwrwrrrr . . ." he breathed. "Come back, damn ye!"

The bitch made a small whimpering yelp and hung back on the rope. He stopped and warned it seriously: "Now, don't ye start makin more trouble for me!" Then he hauled it forward.

Tucking the lapels of his light raincoat together under his chin, he shrugged his shoulders and went on, assessing warily the antics of the raw liquor that yawed through his body. As usual, while the drink only disturbed his sense of balance, it increased the activity of his mind. In fact, such times he would seem to have two heads: one to moil over past misdeeds and failures, while the other was left conveniently free to blow and boast.

Coldly totaling the immediate failures, head number one said, "Well? What's to be done now? You walked into Bob Dowden's dwelling with the greatest of expectations. Was he not the cousin of your dear dead father? Was he not an old rich bachelor with a tidy farm? Instead of politely refusing that half pint of potheen, you had to down it on an empty belly to show what a man you were, and then you sat in with the boys at their twopenny spoilfive."

"Bwrwrwrwrrrr! God damn ye, will ye come here!"

"Talk about all the money you made and your glorious past and the women you had! What did you do? You shamed Dowden out of offering you bed and board this Christmas night, you did. Spoilfive is right! Never could resist a card, could you, or a drink, or a broad? The three of them have followed you with ruin your whole life through."

"Adam Finney has a sense of humor," said head number two.

"Aye! And what'll he do now—kid himself he's in a hotel on a feather bed? Agh!—sitting down and twisting a few poor farmers' boys out'a their few bob, drinking a half gallon of mountain dew to win a half-bred shepherd bitch that he doesn't want. Wonderful!"

"The bitch is worth two pound any time!" the second head defended.

"Bwrwrrrrr!"

"Face up to it, Finney. You're a forgotten exile now, a lost man and a sinner. Time has stolen away your youth. Time is black and heavy upon you. Where are you going to lay your head this night?"

"Agh, whisht now! Ye can go to the sister's place? She'll be glad to see ye, man! Blood's thickern water. She'll welcome ye with open arms—her long-lost black sheep brother home from the world's wilderness. Ye'll be kinda hero!"

"Maryann?" he muttered.

"Like hell you will! She hates your guts. She'll never forgive you."

"Agh!—time heals old sores!" He shrugged.

"In your present state and general decomposition? . . . Adam Finney have you no pride at all? Fifteen long and silent years? Fifteen *dozen* years wouldn't wipe clean your shame with her!"

"Arragh, she's happy now? Dowden says she has a new baby—the third it is. Not bad goin for an old man well past seventy—three alive an three dead. Old man's darlin: that's what she is. But what's wrong to stay with her over Christmas? Christmas is always Christmas an Maryann won't want to mind anything about it now. Stay the night away an leave with decency on the morrow an give the childer the wee bitch for a present from their Uncle Adam."

"Bwrwrwrrrr . . ."

"Aye, Christmas Eve!" number one head said sadly. "What did you come back at all for?"

"I came home, well, because I just damn well *wanted* to come home! Have I not a right to visit the place of me birth?"

"You haven't any rights left, Finney, me boy. You've devoured your rights."

"I'm a proud an a free man yet!"

"You're a bag of bad wind with a terrible sickness on it! You're a blown horse, Finney. You're at your tether's end."

His body shivered, and he broke into a loose cough.

Then he heard the tinkle of running water, and stopped. He wanted a drink. His throat was dry after the potheen. He gazed myopically about and stumbled toward the water sounds, vaguely identifying the place as Templemore, an old monastery destroyed by Cromwell. This would be the overflow from Templemore Well, a famous parish spring that had never admitted a drought.

He groped through the bushes for the beaten footpath, guided by the chirping water as it chuckled over the stones. He remembered the spring, a twelve-by-six-foot cave cut cleanly into the rock under a powerful curve of ashlar. "Come on!" he grunted to the dog, dragging it stiff-legged after him.

He had a healthy respect for the well's depth. He could

not see a thing under the trees. Dropping to his knees, he felt forward to the water's edge and wet his sleeve. Taking off his hat he scooped it full and drank deeply, the water tasting slightly of the sweetness of hair oil.

Satisfied, he sat back on his heels, belching, shaking the hat dry and putting it back on his head, the wet leather band a burning rim of coldness on his brow. The water made him queasy, stirring up the potheen's power again, and small sleety snow began to fall through the drizzle, touching his numb face. He struck a match to see the time, saw the snow falling, and muttered in the double after-darkness, "Snowin now, bigod . . . five to midnight."

The bitch was whining; he could feel her trembling through the rope. "Shut up!" he growled, and waited for a new dizziness to subside. He lit a cigarette, but the first draw made him cough so much he threw the fag away, the smoke blending with the phlegm in his throat and tasting like tar.

He shuddered and got onto his feet. There was an old tale about this spring. Two monks were sometimes seen coming to it in the dead of night, dragging a woman between them, holding her by the arms and pushing her head and shoulders under the water. Some of the old people believed the earth remembered deeds and murders; and Templemore's reputation was doubly unsavory for the well's being on Will Curry's land. Will was an unsociable man.

A shrieking gust caught and would have spilled him, but he dropped to his hands and knees.

Twenty years ago Will had caught Adam progging the orchard with sister Maryann. Only sixteen, she was hipped and breasted like a woman. With her red hair blowing and her milk-white skin, she had a pile of rosy apples gathered in her skirt. She couldn't run with them, and Will caught her, carrying her back under his arm to beneath the tree Adam was in. With her kicking and screaming, he laughed and put her over his knee and pulled down her drawers, skelping her bare arse. *Never forget the sight!*

"Or," Finney cried into the wind, "when I slid down the tree an he grabbed me! I kicked the old goat in the groin, an he got thick and choked me, an I watched everything goin black with a roarin in me ears, but I couldn't tell him to stop.

"When I came to, he was plashin water over me face here at the spring an cryin, 'God, I mighta kilt ye! God, I mighta kilt ye! What hell did ye kick me for?'

"But he give us all the apples we could carry an five bob to boot!"

Later that night he had staggered home, one side of the road the same as the other. Maryann was standing at the fire warming herself in her nightgown. . . .

Only this evening Dowden had said something about Will going sour and wild, taking tramps in off the road to manage for him, setting his house on fire in the horrors of drink, God rest his soul. A terrible rough man he was, Dowden said, able for twenty pints in an evening. But then he had found a hill of gold in Australia.

With a groan, Finney got to his feet and began picking his way back to the road. Snow was falling thickly now, melting on the road but lying on the grass verges and lifting the darkness a little. Now and again he reeled, pulling the dog after him. He tried to breathe shallowly, since a deep breath stabbed his chest like a knife and made him cough. He wanted to cough but kept it back for fear. He had coughed up blood once on the boat.

Finney was crying in his mind now, saying over and over, "Some place to go, some place to go, a place to sleep, a room with a roof, a dry place to lie down, and sleep!"

Trying to keep away from him, the nervous dog looped the rope round his ankles. He blundered, hamstrung, across the road, trying to save himself from falling, hauling at the rope and drawing the terrified animal close to his legs. She unwound the rope again, leaping away the length of it and hawking him headfirst across a low wall. . . .

In the near distance he began to hear a loud voice roaring at cattle. It was old Will Curry's voice, and Finney bestirred himself. Will was waving a hurricane lamp and swearing at half a dozen bullocks as he tried to get them into a shed out of the weather. His excited dog pressed the beasts too hard, and they ran past the door, surging up the muddy lane toward Finney.

Finney stood nervously in the lane's mouth and watched the blowing, shadowy beasts shuffle toward him in the darkness. He yelled and waved his arms and turned them, while Will lifted his lamp over his head, trying to see beyond its dim saucer of light. Reluctantly, Finney shouted for Will to stand below the shed and he would drive them back. The last person he wanted to meet on such a night was old Will Curry.

The lamp ceased its wild gyrations and cast the stilted shadows of Will's legs across the yard's pocked mud, and with Finney behind them the animals huffed suspiciously into the dark shed, the dog flitting back and forth at their heels.

Will slammed the door and turned a large stone on edge against it. He came over, holding up the lamp to Finney's face.

"Arragh, it's ye, Adam!" he roared, and Finney shrank back afraid. "How are ye, man?"

The old man's beery breath was heavy on the air, and his drunken reeling bulk came close to tower over him.

"I'm well, Will," he muttered. "It has turned a bad night." He was thinking he should have allowed the bullocks to find their own way back.

Will was agreeing. "Aye—bad. I'm ony back from the town meself." Will belched and swayed, and Finney watched the snow slant softly past the lamp.

"I'd better be gettin along, Will, before the snow's too thick underfoot."

"Aye," Will agreed absently. Then he looked up and shouted, "Come in for a bit, man?" He reached out and caught Finney's arm with a great square hand that was hard and heavy as an iron ingot. "Come an tell us your travels, man!" he cried, and his great fingers bit into Finney's flesh.

They walked slowly round the end of the dwelling house, Will indifferent to the six-inch soupy cattle-mud sucking at their feet. He was still holding Finney's arm, not steering him so much as leaning on him; demanding to know how many high yallers Finney had coupled. Then he stopped short suddenly to ask in a loud and porter-spittled whisper did Finney know the ruse the aborigine women had used against the miners? "They filt it with sand, bigod!" he answered with a shocked hiss.

Finney had the clear image of a female shaped like a sandglass, and Will mulled on shaking his head and repeating "Sand bigod!" as he led the way round to the front door.

The kitchen was surprisingly tidy, the hearth swept clean with a big bright fire of logs upon it. The scum from a huge three-legged cauldron of potatoes spilled over into the flames, the lid rising and falling with lugubrious sighs. The last time Finney had seen the room it was lit by a solitary candle in a bottle on the table—a filthy bachelor shambles with castoff clothes draped on every chair and a heap of strong socks by the darkened fireside. Now the whitewashed walls seemed lofty, illuminated as they were by the clean double-burner paraffin reflector that hung from a peg on one of them.

Will had aged, his giant's shoulders rounding a little, and his great barrel of a body was much thinner. His face was even lean, and in the fire's flicker it seemed pared down to the bone.

Will's black collie dog had crept through the open door and slunk over near the fire, making itself small in a dim corner and licking its wet paws. Finney did not want to stay and yet was glad of the shelter. While dreading the long laborious trek up snow-covered Templemore Hill and down again, and then across windswept Tullaghmore Bog where green will-o'-the-wisps gamboled and the road quaked underfoot, he wanted to go home. He was about to say that he wanted to go home when Will roared, "Peg?"

In the small room behind the kitchen there was a smooth

and sensual movement. Out came a handsome young woman, red as the queen of diamonds. She was tall and
generous of build but moved with a springy lightness.
Barelegged she was, the old brown shoes on her feet gaping across their cracked toe-creases, and she wore a tight
yellow blouse and a flimsy rag of a green skirt. Her fleshy
calves tapered swiftly to slim round ankles. She reminded
Finney of an old painting he had seen somewhere, and she
also reminded him strongly of his sister, Maryann, who had
been a red-fleshed woman of very similar build.

"Get us a couple stouts," Will ordered.

She met Finney's covering look and let her yellow eyes
run over him as she turned back to the scullery. Her copper-
colored hair was molded into a large mound on the back of
her head above a long and tapered neck. Her sleevebands
bit into the flesh of her upper arms like garters, while her
bare forearms tapered to slim wrists and hands. She reminded him of every woman he had tumbled, and yet he
had never seen her like before, nor could he remember what
she looked like now that she was no longer before him.

Reading his puzzled appreciation, Will said, "She's not
a bad ould hure at all." He carried a chair to the far corner
of the hearth and sat to unlace a dirty boot. "She keeps an
eye on me. An ould man's nights are long an lonely. But
sit ye down, man! Draw up a chair an tell us your travels?"

Finney moved slowly toward a chair, watching Will
anxiously as the dog had done. He caught sight of his own
face in a mirror and started. For a moment he thought it
was himself he saw but younger, with a clear unbroken
eye; but when he took a step closer to the glass, his reflection grew old once more.

"Take a chair, man!" Will demanded, crossing his legs to get at the lace.

Reluctantly Finney moved the chair to the opposite end of the hearth and sat. The fire was very hot. His damp coat and trousers steamed, warming the skin on his legs. He tried to think who this Peg could be. Will had never married. Someone had said that he had kept whores as housekeepers before.

Will—dead? But he was nowhere near dead, sitting there, large, and dangerous as ever, after his usual Saturday spree. Finney decided that he must be getting mixed in his head: it was the effect of the fierce potheen and the fire. It could make a man drunk in several ways. But somehow he did not feel drunk now, and Will was seven-eighths drunk.

Will was lurching over the bootlace, saliva falling in little spiderwebs from his mouth. "Tell us about your travels, man?" he grumbled. He dropped his foot, boot and all, on the floor and swayed several times toward the fire, turning his head from the heat. Obediently, Finney searched his head, unable to find much worth the telling.

"Montreal it was," he began. "It was in Montreal, and I half-dead with the cold an coughin like a horse. I met up with a deck hand who'd jumped ship to Liverpool. When I got there, the cops were waitin for the guy whose name I had, but I slipped them since I looked nothin like him, an anyway, I had me own passport."

Will still worked on the bootlace, his chair tipped forward on its front legs as he bent over. He was not listening. The savor of the boiling potatoes made Finney realize he was hungry. He had not had a feed like that for years.

"Go on!" said Will, absently.

"Then I came back home—yesterday, it was. Aye, yesterday. I guess that's about all," he said shortly. It was as though he had sung for supper.

Then Peg slipped in with two glasses and four bottles of stout. She glanced contemptuously at Will's hunched form as she set them on the table. A swift and secret smile for Finney drifted across her lips. At high-breasted puberty with her long swan neck and sloping shoulders, Peg would have been like the young half-caste girl he had taken that time. Will might like to hear that.

"I noticed her in the town," he said in a low voice. "It was in Texas—near Houston. A green slip of a dress on her plump little body, an I follered her out of the town in the dusk."

Oddly, Will was not interested. He got rid of the first stubborn boot and glanced sideways at Peg and the bottles.

"Pull them for us," he said.

She reached over across the table, opened and rummaged through a small drawer for a corkscrew. She could have handier moved round the table but leaned over and let her two breasts ride up out of the blouse. Finney stared, thinking how the young half-white's breasts had looked.

With an eye on its master, Will's dog arose and crept round the room by the walls to Peg and tried to lick her hand, but she ignored it.

Will's efforts with the second boot were very slow. The fire had made him drowsy, but when the stout gurgled in the glasses he reached a hand out sideways. Peg placed a glass in it, and brought the second one to Finney, standing in so close to him that her body brushed against his knees.

"Here's health, avic!" Will called, opening his mouth and slinging in the liquid.

Normally to Finney a bottle of stout was a good thing, but he did not want this one. He frowned, casting about for a place to dump it. In the firelight it winked as red as blood, its foamy head like froth in a slaughterhouse drain. The thought sickened him.

Will stood the empty glass on the floor and carried on clumsily with the stubborn boot. Peg stood by the table fiddling with the corkscrew, forcing Finney to be aware of her, while the dog sat on its haunches under the table looking up. Absently, she slipped her left foot out of its shoe and scratched its belly. It caught at her leg with its canine mating grip, and she held out the leg to it.

Although all this pantomime seemed unaware and point-less, Finney knew it was for his benefit. It moved slightly the lust of his body but left him undisturbed. He wanted to be away. He had some place to go. . . .

"I have to go home, Will," he said aloud. "They'll be expecting me . . ." Neither Will nor Peg gave any sign they heard him.

"They . . . ?" he asked himself. Who were they? And then he had no home, never making one. No one was ex-pecting him. No one even knew he was alive. He would get warm and dry at the fire and maybe get a feed of floury spuds and then get up and go. They could not hinder him.

Suddenly Peg spurned the dog, startling him, throw-ing it onto its back as though she had divined his indifference. She stared straight into his eyes. Her eyes were topaz-yellow, the firelight firing them as flames flickering, as knives flashing. Two hot hollows in her head they were, burning, but also dead. He met her eyes, pretending to plot with her, smiling and shaking his head quickly at the untouched stout in his hand, and she nodded understandingly.

Neatly, she picked Will's glass off the floor, just bending a knee slightly in her walk and lifting the glass in a single flowing motion as she came to Finney. She handed him the empty glass and took the full one, her hand reached above the rim and holding it close to her skirt as she passed back to the table behind Will.

"Haugh!" Will snorted, jerking back to life. "Pull us another, Peg!"

"No, Will!" Finney protested. "One's enough."

"Arragh, not all, man!" Will insisted. "Do ye good!"

Peg glanced from one to the other, the dog licking her ankles.

"Pull him one!" Will ordered. He snapped the bootlace in irritation and dropped the boot to the floor. Finney felt the small taut pain of the snap in his chest, and Will spread his feet out in relief. Peg came to Finney for the empty glass.

"I've several hures of corns," Will was complaining, "Never get a bloody boot to fit me now."

He wiggled his toes inside the socks, and then decided to take the right sock off, rolling it down from the elastic cuff of his white underpants and peeling it off.

Finney stared at the exposed foot. He could not see it properly but it seemed without flesh, the delicate bones and sinews without skin or cushioning muscle. When Will flexed the foot, the bones made the sound of turning pebbles. Finney felt sick, disbelieving his sight and blaming it. Men could not live and walk about on fleshless feet and next complain of corns; and Finney began to sweat.

"Aye—what about that little Jap cailín ye had in Chicago?" said Will, drawing the sock on again.

Finney sat up in surprise. He could not remember mentioning this girl (nor even the little Mexican girl in San Pedro).

"She was a Filipino," he corrected. "I thought she was a Jap, but the papers said she was a Filipino. I followed her down the street. A cop was coming up an I waited by a burned-out house. She came back with groceries and suckin an ice cream. There was an El going past at the time. She wasn't a Jap. She was a Filipino. . . ."

"No matter, no matter," said Will contentedly. "Put their heads in a bag, an they all look alike, avic."

Finney chuckled. He kept seeing the olive face of the girl.

"I didn't hurt her," he explained. "I did it like the guy in the movies. Don't be blamin me, Will? I—I was terrible lonely, so I just tried to live my own way."

Will was staring into the fire, and Finney could not say if he were listening or not. He glanced at Peg. The changing firelight made her face ovoid and lean and gave her the features of the Filipino girl. Smiling, she turned to the table.

*Pop* went the corks, the sharp sounds jarring Finney to the depths of his body. As if alive, the stout spewed from the bottle necks. With her right hand Peg filled the empty glass and drank Finney's from her left, then filled and delivered two full glasses. As she returned past Will, the old man reached for her roughly.

Looking into Finney's eyes, she gave to his pull, and Finney felt ashamed for Will and the woman, even for himself. He knew Will wanted to name the woman, to boast about her and condemn her. And all the while Will's arm was tightening around her, pulling her against him. Her eyes never left Finney's face, and the dog crept out from under the table, wagging its tail and whining.

"She's not a bad old hure, is Peg," said Will.

His fingers haunched a handful of the skirt and skin on her belly and she winced.

"Washes, darns, cooks. . . ." He laughed.

Inwardly disgusted, Finney forced himself to snicker, and the dog heard and came over to look into his face. He wanted to get up but was powerless to leave his chair. His blood seemed set on fire. It surged through his body in sickening waves.

"She's a good traveler, bigod," Will was saying, and Finney pressed back against the chair to steady himself.

He had never had such a sensation of lightness, and had to hold himself down by hooking a hand under the chair. In so doing, the glass of stout in his left hand tipped, and some of the liquid spilled onto his knee where it made an ice-cold patch. He took a mouthful but could not swallow it, holding it in his mouth and swilling it round his teeth until it grew warm and salty as blood. Will and the woman were now in grotesque embrace.

"Hegh, hegh, hegh!" Will laughed.

"I want to go," Finney tried to say. "I must get away."

"By God, she can carry me!" Will crowed. "Can't ye, Peg, asthore?"

Peg smiled a demure cat smile, self-satisfied as a purr. Her empty yellow eyes had blazed at Finney the entire time, and he thought, "She has something to tell me. That's why she watches me."

"Look ye, avic!" Will bawled. "She has the best backside in the country!"

He dropped his free hand, gathering the skirt into his fist and hoisting it. But it was the cruelty of the hand as it lay upon the fire-touched softness of the woman's belly that fascinated Finney. The hand was now a claw and, as the foot had been, fleshless and hard as a hawk's talon. Then the skirt fell back as Peg pivoted suddenly and moved away, and Will roared in senseless laughter.

His laughter rippled the thickening air like the shatter of a stone in a pool, and Finney peered across the fire at the two of them as though through the opacity of water. Still laughing, Will threw down the second glass of stout. First he spluttered, then erupted in a gasping spasm that forced the liquid through his nostrils and down over his chin. He coughed and snorted, his hands fluttering in the watery air like a drowning man.

Unmoved, Peg stood by the table, the excited dog cowering by her feet. Finney felt vaguely sorry for her while knowing she did not need nor ask for pity.

"Pouff!" Will cried. His wind at least was back, and he was shaking his head. Peg's eyes moved slowly over him. The room was quiet now, and the lid on the pot of potatoes gave a single dying sigh.

Although his front was scorched, Finney's back was chill, the fire's convection drawing the cold air off the night. He looked up, and there seemed no top to the house. There was snow drifting past, caught momentarily in the light.

"Why don't ye go to bed, Will?" Peg advised. She came over for Will's empty glass and whipped Finney's away as before.

"Whaaaa?" said Will, looking craftily at Finney.

Peg shrugged. Pushing three fingers and the thumb of her right hand into the necks of the empty bottles, and nipping the full and empty glasses together with her left hand, she glided into the scullery. Finney heard the squeal, groan, and suck of a pump as she rinsed the glasses.

Will settled himself in his chair, muttering and frowning.

Finney cleared his throat and said as firmly as he dared, "I have to be going now, Will."

"Whaaaa?" Will asked. "Haugh!" he snorted, understanding. "Time enough, man! There's allus enough time for everything."

A log rolled off another's burning back in a pretty shower of sparks, darkening the hearth. The light's new illusion made Will appear as a full skeleton. His domed head teetered on the neck column, and his jaw fixed itself to an awful permanent grin. Finney shuddered, trying to make the sign of the cross, and Will called absently, "Peg? Make up the fire."

She came over from the scullery door and kneeled down on the hearth, beautiful now in the diffused light, taking a pair of tongs with delicate queenly gesture and re-laying the fire's cone, building in some new logs and carefully picking up each little red eye of charcoal.

The collie rose, stretched, cocked its leg against the table leg, and came over to Finney, snuggling its stone-cold nose into his left hand, then going over lazily to Peg.

It stood by her shoulder. She was reclining, leaning on her left arm facing the fire, her breasts leaning one on the other to her left side, her right hand inert on her right thigh, so still and relaxed that the fire's false flames made her at once small and large, visible and invisible, a torso that rested one moment in the earth and the very next disclosed a shadowed, rounded form without humanity. The dog tried to lick her face, and the fire said she was a dog-headed being cut on a shadow-frieze and as old as time.

She moved her head and pushed the beast away with her right hand, then fondled and teased it absently at arm's length.

Will stared unblinkingly into the fire, and he hummed, "I tore me ould britches goin over the ditches to you, Maryann, to you, Maryann . . ."

It was an old folk ditty that Finney had heard as a boy. It had a light lilting tune. "What's the rest of that, Will?" he asked.

There was no reply as Will stared on into the fire. The dog lay now with its head on Peg's thigh. The big pot was boiling dry, and an unpleasant smell was beginning to fill the room.

Behind Will there came another woman, an aborigine and brown almost to blackness with dark and bestially yearning eyes and two strong scars or caste marks cut into each cheek on either side of the broad flat nose and two rows of beadlike scars across her chest above the roots of her low leathery breasts. Her hands were held behind her back. She was quite naked and seemed young. She moved closer to the old man, looking down on his head with a terrible intensity of inarticulate love, and fear, and pity. Will seemed to sense her presence and shrugged uncomfortably, glancing unwillingly to the side.

"Peg?" he muttered, putting out a hand to feel for her.

The hand moved in an arc through the aborigine's body, his eyes following the gesture into their corners so that his bloodshot bulging gray eyeballs filled their sockets like one who was quite sightless or was dead.

Shuddering violently, he said "Haugh!" and Peg broke into a brazen trill of a laugh that raced round the room and fled outside to join the wind's wild laughter.

"Quiet!" Will roared.

"Go to bed!" she chided.

"Aye," he muttered, crestfallen. "Aye, bed. . . ."

The dog went to him and whined, sniffing round the dark woman's bare feet. Will cursed at it, his eyes refusing to look sideways. With bowed head the native woman went away, and her hands were tied with rope behind her back, the crease of the backbone and the two mounds of the shoulder bones stamped momentarily by the fire magic into the form of a cross. Finney chuckled hysterically, thinking about an ass.

"The cross of an ass," he said aloud. "Steal the cross off an ass. . . ."

It was a country saying to denote a real rogue. Scraps of religion Finney had learned and discarded were coming back to him—the great ride on the ass up to the city, then the spittle and the tied hands, Peter cowering by the fire saying "No no" in his long Jewish shirt like Maryann crying by the fire.

With a brief flicker of life Will sat up and stretched. He looked over at Finney.

Embarrassed and scared, Finney said, "Tell us the rest of Maryann, Will?"

"Maryann she want a man, her babby needs a daddio!"

"No!" Finney shouted. "No no!"

Peg laughed wildly again, opening her mouth, her red tongue bunched behind her white lower teeth.

"Oh, husha—husha!" Will complained, shaking his head. "This is a most distressful country, man! The dear ould shamrock's lawless, now. Have ye seen Tandy?"

"Tandy?" Finney asked.

Peg started to sing softly into the fire: "I'ee met wid Napper Tandy an I tuk him be the han—now tell me how is Ire-lan an how diz she stan. . . ." Will dropped his chin on his chest and smiled contentedly. Peg forgot the words and hummed the verse out.

The burned pot was now making black snakes of smoke that writhed and curled like ropes round the room, binding the three of them together in a stinking web. The smell made Finney want to vomit.

Will was remembering:

"Maryann she found the man to dance upon her diddio
And got a father for her bairn, her pore wee laddio."

"Go to bed!" Peg said impatiently.

"I'll be going," Finney said. He was feigning noncha-lance and trying but failing to rise, as though the sour

smoke-ropes now bound him to his seat. There was a dull
moist pounding pain in his chest; and he pressed his back
against the chair to lean away from it.

Will grunted, nodding, and stiffly rose to his feet. Peg
got to her knees on the hearth, unnecessarily putting her
two hands on Finney's knees to assist her rising.

"Do ye want anythin to ate, Will?" she asked with a
smirk.

"No," he said, shaking his head. "The dead can't enjoy
their food an their board is allus empty. They may ony
sleep. Quiet sleep does be a good thing."

He yawned, rubbing a numb hand over his thick-
thatched gray head and, peering down on Finney, asked
suspiciously, "What's he doin' here?"

"Who?" Peg asked.

"Oh," he said secretly, "I thought I saw somethin. I
keep thinkin I see things about me. I keep drinkin pints
I swallowed long ago. In the town this day I saw a tall fair
woman, but a pickle of corn formed her mouth an her two
diddies slapped together like clappers fit to fright crows.
Aye. . . ."

He lumbered to the door, domestically undoing his vest
and top fly buttons and yawning. Opening the door, he
peered out and urinated over the threshold into the night.
A coldness came into the room, a solid ice-block of tangible cold the same shape and size as the door. Outside there
was darkness with snow-flowers dropping through the oblong of light. The falling snow reminded Finney of something he should tell Will.

"I was sheltering in an office doorway," he whispered.
"The snow was thick in the air. Thousands of people were

coming out of work an hurrying into the snow with their heads down. Goin home, they were, to warm bright places. A girl in a white mackintosh came past me. She stood on the step an complained about the snow. Then she turned and smiled at me before she went off. I followed her. She cut across the park. The park was a quiet wilderness of snow, but she screamed when I caught her an a big cop came runnin . . ."

"Where's the wind from?" Peg called, her back to the fire and her two open hands with the backs to her behind to keep the heat off.

"Wind?" Will asked. "No wind," he said, looking around, "just snow fallin. No wind moren the sigh of a worm in the soil . . ."

"Oh," Peg said. "It must be somebody cryin in the night I heard."

Will closed the door, but the snow continued to fall into the room now, hissing into the fire with small swift secret hisses, and the fire was afraid now of dying and caught the flakes with hot anger. He came slowly across the room, muttering, a sprinkling of snow on his head and shoulders. "Not a bad night—not a bad night at all for to die."

"Die?" Finney whispered. "Who said anythin bout dyin, man? Chrisake, let me out'a here!"

"Don't let him moider ye," Peg advised kindly. "He does think deep things in his age. The world is allus full of wild words an sleep, avic. Go to bed, Will? Go to bed an say your prayers."

"I mind—I mind the time when the whole wide world was a wildflower of goold in me hand," he said hesitatingly and sadly. "I mind—I mind the cailíns skippin along the roads. People moved with a dance in their legs them days . . ."

"Husha, now!" Peg scolded, taking his heavy right arm and turning him to face the steep stairs. "It's the wooden hills an blanket valleys for ye, avic!"

"This wide world's a broken pore place now," Will said. "An ould bedstead wid rusty springs . . . aye. Bed for the gettin, bed for the birthin, an bed for the dyin away . . ."

"Oh, husha, husha!" Peg said again, shaking his arm. "Ye'd jaw the crow off the corncock! Bed an prayers!"

"Aye, bed an prayers," Will said forlornly, "the bread an butter of life . . ."

On weighted feet he moved to the stairs, starting in a hopeful, childish treble to say, "Now, I lay me down to sleep, I pray the Lord me soul to keep . . ."

Peg came back and lifted the lamp off the wall and followed him, the light fanning mysteriously about her face, casting small shadows off its contours into its hollows and making her Mary meek and beautiful. With slow creaking steps Will climbed, his feet dropping on each step like stones, and ahead of him Finney could see no end to the long stairway as though it slanted into space and rode up into the lost darkness of the night. ". . . wake I at morn or wake I never . . ."

On the floor above, their feet pounded and shuffled as though they were making heavy songless dance, the wind now a single nervous note on a single string seeking like a whining dog around the house. The collie dog came over to Finney and lay down by his feet for company.

Without the lamp the fire failed to master the shadows

which took possession of the kitchen up to the hot edge of the hearthstone, and Finney watched the light and shadow warriors writhe in silent struggle—cowering, crouching, leaping, lunging.

The pot was making as much fume as a factory chimney, and he gasped laboring for a clean breath, the bulbous cords of smoke twisting about the room.

He tried to move off the chair by putting his weight on his arms. When he stood with great effort, the floor reeled like the deck of a boat. "Home now," he thought, "the black backs of the Donegal hills on the dawn sky."

Against Will's mumbling prayers Peg started to sing: "They dressed me up in scarlet red an treated me very kindly but I could not forget the girl that I'ee left behin me . . ."

"Quiet!" Will roared like a blow. "Quiet, ye blasphemous bitch!"

Although his body ran with sweat, Finney tucked by habit the lapels of his coat under his chin. The talk and fumbling upstairs had ceased, and the bed complained as Will lay down on it, and then Peg laughed her high wild laugh. So wild was it that it might have been a blast of wind across the chimney, and the dog lifted its head and gave a long wailing call that sent a shiver down Finney's back.

"Where—where am I at all?" he whispered, gazing around and seeing the room now with a white snow layer over everything.

Fixing his eyes on the distant door, he moved slowly toward it and had a hand on the latch when he heard Peg's voice softly behind him.

"Ye're not goin?" she asked as though surprised.

He could just barely see her outline against the fire's decreasing cone, her hands on her hips, her elbows sticking out like jug handles. He moved his thick tongue over his lips.

"Ye're not feered of me?" she challenged.

"No," he whispered.

"What ails ye, then?"

He did not know what to say.

"This night is young an quiet as t'grave now," she said like a purr, glancing sideways at the stairs. "Come on—if ye're a man at all!"

She lifted the hem of her skirt above her knees, moving her body in a poor gesture of allurement, offering herself as women across the world offered themselves to men one way or another. The old broken shoes slapping up and down on her heels, she made a little dance and sang: "O lovely Maryann! Me gentle little swan! Where'er I bee I'll dream of thee, till life's last pulse is gone. . . ."

"Shut up!" he said, choking. "Ye're a witch—a bloody witch! A witch is what ye are! A witch . . ." He kept saying witch, unable to stop.

Peg laughed, and the dog came to her, whining and wagging its tail. She held out her foot to it, balancing on the right one and teasing it as she had done before.

"I'm sick," Finney complained. She was playing a clever game, and he saw through it. If he started on her she would kill him. "I'd—I'd be no good to ye," he muttered in mock ashame. She laughed in her throat, richly and proudly, flinging the dog away.

Upstairs in a dream Will shouted, "Haugh!" the bed

creaking like a wind-tormented door. "Git t'hell away from me!" he roared. "Byegone is byegone—let t'dead bury t'dead for God's sake!"

"Ye wouldn't be feered of the pore old man?" she asked, innocently.

Taking his hand off the latch, he turned back. "Tell me, is he dead?" he said.

She gave her wild loud laugh, throwing back her head and opening her mouth.

"Stop laughin at me!" he shouted, the strength of his shout starting a cough deep in his throat, and blood came to the corners of his mouth. She waited politely till he ceased, and said slowly:

"What is death? Everything lives for the dead an the deeds of the living are the food of the dead an dead men are free fancy men, no bargain binds them. They sing in their dreams an live in the morrow. Come—don't be freckened."

She reached forward gently and took his left arm, leading him over to the fire across the snow-powdered floor. She kneeled on the hearth, drawing him down beside her, saying softly, "Ah musha, musha—a fire is a grand thing . . ."

They watched the fire. It was dying, the heavy snow-flakes sizzling on the red-bright logs and freckling the mass with black dead stains. "The snow's killin the fire," Peg said, sadly. "I've often wondered where fire does be when it dies. Fire's a quare thing. . . ."

She held his right hand firmly and comfortingly in her left. "I've waited the long time till ye come back. I never forgot . . ."

She turned her body to him, putting her two hands on his shoulders and pushing him down so he was flat on the hearth. Kneeling beside him, she pushed the dog away when it scrabbled across his body and tried to lick her face. Leaning over him, she grasped his wrists and lifted them above his head, pinning them to the floor, pressing her heavy weight of breast upon his chest. The dog kept moving round them. "Lew!" she commanded. "Lew—lie down!"

"No—no!" Finney wheezed, unable to draw a full breath with the weight of her. With a great effort he wrenched free his hands and tried to push her away. He could not move her and for an eternity he tensed his body against her, sweating and panting and whispering: "No! No! No! No!"

Upstairs the bed squeaked and they heard a gurgling cough. The bed creaked loudly again, and a heavy form blundered onto the floor along with the musical shattering of glass. The dog sat on its haunches and started a low long tenor yowl in its throat rising and falling in a minor key. . . .

Finney was puzzled. Peg's body was not soft. It was hard —hard and heavy as a boulder crushing down on him. In a wild rage he grasped at her breasts and they were cold and soft as snow. He buried his fingers in them, filling his fists with them and the handfuls came away, the flesh white and cold like snow, and the dog, barking sharply now, started tugging at his sleeve.

Peg's face still wore a smile—not a triumphant nor a satisfied smile: an ancient, motiveless, sexless smile unanswerable and unceasing. Gathering his strength he flung her away, craving every breath but scared to draw the air too deeply. He shut his eyes and concentrated on the breathing, jealously feeding the air in little mouthfuls into his aching lungs.

When he opened his eyes the whole room was white and the fire had gone out, the dog still shivering and whining beside him. Then he saw Will standing on the bottom step of the stairs in what seemed a long white nightshirt, his face gray and vacant and calm.

Finney was dead scared now. Will could kill him. "No —no," he whispered, cowering down on the floor beside the dog. Will paid no attention and walked over to the door which swung open before him, letting in a clear cool wind that churned up the choking smoke rings and blew them away.

To Finney the room now seemed wall-less as a sea, a white sea without bound or border. He stood up, his weariness gone. Will was standing with his right hand up-raised in a sign of benediction and acceptance, and then he beckoned with the left hand.

"Will . . .?" Finney whispered, not sure whether the figure was Will or not.

Then, looking down on the dog, he moved away from it without effort, a great lightness in him, and he knew he was free at last to leave earth, earthlust, lifelust and lust behind. Swiftly he followed the white figure out into the vast coenobium of the night that listened to the song of church bells caroling for Christmas Day. . . .

The Christmas morning a neighbor who had been at Bob Dowden's card party told the Poyntzes that Adam was back in the old country and acting like a millionaire. Maryann took the news quietly—it seemed little more than a waking day continuation of a dream she had had the night before about her brother and herself in childhood: one of a thousand dreams, the old event unburied and working through the lagan of her soul.

The children were stirred, the vagueness round their uncle's existence clothing him in a heroic glamour. Poyntz was in short humor. The snow had slowed his morning chores. They were all likely to be late for church. He was a one thing at a time man and small crises always upset him.

He bundled the harness on the cob and led it to the trap, calling: "Hasten, there! Hasten, now!" impatiently nibbling his lower lip with its tiny goatbeard of gray hair as they climbed in, and driving off before they were settled.

The children were wide-eyed at the blizzard's transformation of the old green land, its cracks and scars healed by a salve of snow, each aching angle filled with a fillet of snow, the tree boles rinded with snow, their leafless branches pointing to the pale-blue sun-bright sky: snow was a seldom thing and when it came so well it was a miracle.

Maryann said nothing, holding her last baby in her arms, looking with inscrutable gaze at the plain craggy features of her husband, a man full forty years her senior, and wondering about her brother.

The cob made its own pace on the slippery road, it refused to hasten and Poyntz was nervous it might go down. He kept clicking his tongue and fussing with the reins, trying to pick rough patches in the road ahead and denying the cob the full use of its own wisdom. The church bell began to ring. It would ring for twenty minutes and to be in time they should have passed Knock Crossroads and not be a half mile below it. Poyntz could see the church spire's black finger across the white fields and fretted, nibbling his lip. He was strict about church matters and would sooner turn back from the door than disturb a service.

The snow hurt his dull eyes and he was weary after a heavy morning's work shoveling the drifts round the buildings. At Templemore overhanging trees had kept the snow soft and the cob was able to trot. Then young John shouted, startling them all:

"Daddo! Daddo! There's a dog! We've passed a black shepherd dog, daddo!"

Maryann and young Mary followed the boy's imperious pointing.

Poyntz scowled, not looking around and muttering: "Never mind! Never mind!"

"It's on a rope, daddo! It's tied to a rope!"

Poyntz glanced at his wife, who nodded agreement with the boy, but he said, shrugging distastefully: "Leave it be! We're late as it is!"

"But it's tied to somethin, daddo!" the boy protested tearfully. "It's caught! Let me go get it? You go on an I'll catch ye?"

"Be still or ye'll toss the cob!" Poyntz ordered, but knowing his mother was with him, the boy had already flung off the rug and was clambering over the trap door. The shifting weight upset the cob and it slid nervously to a halt.

"Whoa!" Poyntz cried helplessly. "Stay where ye are, damn it!"

But young John was away down the road, clots of snow flying over his back.

The little bitch whined gladly, leaning on the rope and trying to lick his hand, her thin body a constant shiver.

"Good bitch—good bitch," he encouraged softly, putting a hand on her head and running his fingers down the frost-stiff rope and then pulling on the rope to free it and lifting up what looked like a gnarled bit of a branch.

But it was not a branch, and although unwilling to accept his eyes' evidence the boy saw a gray human hand in a sleeve clawed round a small pellet of pink snow, a gray hand on a wood-stiff wrist and a coral egg of frozen snow in it, pink snow like the icing on his mother's Christmas cake. . . .

He dropped the rope and the hand dropped back. His eyes swiftly measured the dimensions of the snowy mound, the awful mound soiled and trampled by the dog's restless paws.

A long way off they were waiting in the trap—watching from the trap a thousand miles away, his father beckoning impatiently. He tried to shout but his voice only made a whisper. The dog licked his bare knees. He waved with both arms and heard his father ask: "What hell's wrong wid him?"

The boy pointed to the ground and waved again. Maryann turned back the rug, opened the trap door and got out. The boy saw her actions with a relief he would never forget; her coming to him down the road on the soft snow verge, the baby in her arms, her breath making little clouds about her head, a dead oak beyond her with crooked fingers crying to the sky: he could hardly wait and yet remain alive. . . . Oh, hasten, hasten.

When she was near he whispered: "It's a man, ma?" asking her if she knew and hoping he was wrong. "The dog's tied to it . . ."

Maryann stood above the mound, her bright frost-fired face going sallow. "God save us," she whispered, looking down into her son's eyes. "Some poor man got caught in the storm," she added protectively against the boy's terror, his fear-opened features shocking her they looked so like his uncle's.

"Get daddo," he was saying hoarsely.

In the trap Poyntz chewed his lower lip, acutely conscious of the hurrying bell, but in answer to his wife's summons he climbed out and went to the cob's head, telling the Mary child to hold the reins as he turned the animal and led it back, calling crossly: "What hell's up—we're surely late now!"

When he saw the hand and the mound he removed his hard hat, his white bald head waxen in the sun. He was shocked, but said practically: "Don't stir anythin. We'll have to tell the po-lice."

But John refused to leave the dog behind: no more than he could stay there himself could he leave the dog nor bear to think and think of it being there nightlong, nightlong tethered to a dead man's hand. . . .

Poyntz could not bring himself to touch the hand and slip the dull off the wrist, so he cut the noose from the dog's neck. He was curious about the man but did not want to remove the shroud of snow before the children. . . .

"What is it?" Mary called from the trap.

"Nothin—nothin," he grumbled, nodding to wife and son to come away and frightened in himself—five years beyond the Abrahamic span, a death diminished his own slow-running sand.

John lifted the bitch, sobbing in his chest with pity and shock. They put it in the warm well of the trap between their legs under the rug and started off again.

"We can call the po-lice from t'Rect'ry," Poyntz said, still thinking about church although the service would be half over when they got that far.

Maryann watched her son and to soothe his mind said conversationally: "That's old Will Curry's place."

They all glanced at the roofless house and tumbled steadings, their gaunt starkness trebled by the bland snow's perfection.

The baby started to cry, singing ah-lah, ah-lah, ah-lah and kicking with each syllable. Maryann shushed it and started to undo her coat, fumbling in her blouse for a breast and clamping the child's face against it and holding it there, her hand palmed over the back of its baby-bald head. It sucked strongly and guttered in its napkin. Young John heard it and thought how bothersome babies were. He could feel the great nervous shudders of the bitch against his legs. They could all feel the shudders moving coldly through their bodies.

"Will Uncle Adam be at the church?" Mary asked.

"We'll see," Maryann replied shortly.

"It's odd he didn't come over," Poyntz said as though the idea had just struck him. Maryann did not reply.

She fed the child and watched her boy, seeing afresh the

great likeness to his uncle. He was fourteen now, although he looked and acted more like ten, a gentle quiet lad with little sign of wildness. Oh, she watched him closely for any sign of wildness, and the neighbors kept saying: My oh my, is he not the pure Finney!

Well, why not—since he was pure Finney. No one knew that and no one would ever know.

The church bell had stopped for five minutes before Poyntz heard the silence of it. He glanced at his wife and saw a strange woman with hard tawny eyes in a set stony face. Had he been able to see in the dark her expression would have been familiar, but this was the first time she had betrayed it in daylight.

She was looking at him, through him, past him, mercilessly unseeing him as a man at all, neither as husband nor as human being; seeing a toothless old hag-hulk of a man, guileful and gullible, an old goat-lusty bag-o'-bones bald man. . . . But she did not hate him at all, she only despised him while fond of him in an odd way, and could thole him as many a woman bore with many a man, many a worse or better man, good or bad making little difference: and Poyntz was much like a boy now, his fumbling passion swift and shy as a boy's.

No—hate she reserved for her brother Adam, a cold glazed time-fired stone of hate lying secretly in her heart for his witless useless action, sin neither here nor there, that had given her for once the pain of pleasure and the pleasure of terror on a drunken lawless whim, and then condemned her to a slow life of frustration alongside an old man with age-cold, age-flabby skin, day eking day, night borrowing night, dream denying dream. She looked at her son, praying a desperate secret prayer, asking that he should not be wild or queer, that she should learn to love him less, but never learn to hate him as she lived lonely in the ritual prison of her regret.

Concentrating on the ground ahead of the cob's fore-feet, Poyntz asked, "What's wrong?"

After a silence she answered untruthfully but with more truthfulness than she divined: "I was thinkin about that pore man. . . ."

Young John slipped a hand down under the rug and touched the bitch's wet head and felt the grateful tongue licking him. He could still see the snow-embalmed hand, a gray talon jessed to the shivering dog fawning in utter gratitude before him, the autochthonous hand raising it-self out of the snow. Come Christmas with or without snow, come snow in January or in May, he would always see the hand and feel the heaviness of it on a frozen rope. . . .

## ABOUT THE AUTHOR

Anthony C. West was born in 1910 in County Downs, Ireland. During his childhood and youth, he spent as much time as he could camping out in the lake country. He disliked school. His restlessness eventually led him to thoughts of emigration. He flipped a coin to decide whether his destination would be America or Australia. America won, and in 1930 he arrived in New York, unaware of the depression and not much caring: his object was to wander, not to make money. Wander he did, from New York across the country to the Pacific Northwest, which he loved, supporting himself with an amazing variety of temporary or migratory jobs, mostly farm labor.

However, he found in himself a consuming desire to go home and in 1938 returned to a Europe about to go to war. He served in the Air Force and was navigator of the lead plane in the Mosquito Bomber missions of Germany. Since the war he has lived on a farm in Anglesey, North Wales. He deeply loves his beautiful but barren land—enough to struggle constantly to eke a living out of its thin, rocky soil for his wife and nine children.

West works with the relentless intensity of a man who began writing late and must catch up. Besides his short story writing, he is working on a novel and has another projected. Of his work he writes: "I am not interested in describing the wrinkles in my particular soul—I want to play on world themes, to paint the macrocosm in the microcosm." Thus also the powerful, dramatic writing on nature in these stories finds its creative roots in the magnificence of the Northwest and the great plains of Canada, in the endless, ever-changing configurations of cloudscapes to which he became almost addicted during years of flying, and especially in the bleak beauty of Ireland and Wales.

83/
85